ABOUT DARK HART COLLECTION

THE DARK HART COLLECTION is a line of novels and novellas curated by me, Sadie Hartmann, aka "Mother Horror," for Dark Matter INK. These stories map new territories in the ever-evolving landscape of the horror genre. I invite you to escape into books written by authors who blur the lines between multiple genres, and who explore the depth and breadth of dark hearts everywhere.

Sincerely,

Sadie Hartmann

Sadie Hartmann
Curator, The Dark Hart Collection

PRAISE FOR MOSAIC

"A masterful blend of folk and cosmic horror, woven together under the craft of stained glass restoration. Mosaic is a masterpiece."

—Tim McGregor, author of *Lure* and *Wasps in the Ice Cream*

"*Mosaic* reeks of dread and the creeping suspicion that something's watching you. It's full of suspense that propels the narrative, and mysteries that whisper long after the story ends. I loved this book."

—Steph Nelson, author of *The Vein*

"*Mosaic* is a great story, told by a deft writer. It's dark, it's brooding, and it'll have you on the edge of your seat."

—Ross Jeffery, Bram Stoker Award-nominated author of *The Devil's Pocketbook*

"A novel spilling over with mystery, cosmic terror, and radiant color. Catherine McCarthy's *Mosaic* is a special kind of descent straight into Hell."

—C. S. Humble, author of *That Light Sublime Trilogy* and *The Black Wells Series*

MOSAIC

Copyright © 2023 Catherine McCarthy

This book is a work of fiction. Any reference to historical events, real people, or real places are used fictitiously. Other names, characters, places, and events are products of the author's or artist's imagination, and any resemblance to actual events or places or persons, living or dead, is entirely coincidental.

All rights reserved. No part of this book may be reproduced or used in any manner without the prior written permission of the copyright owner, except for the use of brief quotations in a book review.

Edited by Marissa van Uden
Book Design and Layout by Rob Carroll
Cover Art and Design by Devin Forst

ISBN 978-1-958598-06-1 (paperback)
ISBN 978-1-958598-43-6 (eBook)
ISBN 978-1-958598-44-3 (audiobook)

darkmatter-ink.com

MOSAIC

CATHERINE MCCARTHY

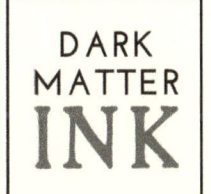

DARK
MATTER
INK

To Tony...always.

ONE

THE LETTER ARRIVES by snail-mail, addressed to Mr. R. Griffiths, which raises my hackles. Robin Griffiths, the name on my website states, and because I'm a glazier, people assume I'm male. However, I refuse to add a profile photo to the site, because my gender has nothing whatsoever to do with my profession.

I tear the letter open, wreaking revenge on the envelope, and skip to the valediction. The correspondent is the Chairman of Bilbury Parish Council, a Mr. Jonathan Hargreaves. Not Chair or Chairperson—Chair*man*. That might explain the gender assumption.

This is the first time a potential client has contacted me by letter in a long time. I massage the bridge of my nose, thinking how much simpler it would have been for both of us had he used the website submission form. He must have found me via my website, so why didn't he choose to email? Now I'm expected to reply by the same means, as he has not included an email address or telephone number.

I'm tempted to bin the letter, but the words "*deconsecrated thirteenth-century church*" and "*woodland setting*" leap from the page, making the contents too appetizing to ignore. Propped on a stool at the breakfast bar, I dunk a second chocolate biscuit in my tea and devour the whole four pages.

BACK IN THE studio, I set to work with the soldering iron. The project I'm working on demands little focus, and my mind wanders in the direction of the church window that Jonathan Hargreaves wants restored.

His enthusiasm for the project had oozed from the page. He'd written that they intended to use the church not only as a place of worship *for all faiths and denominations* (though how successful that will be I can only imagine), but also as a community center with a variety of arts and social clubs on offer. There was also the Lottery grant, as well as a substantial sum raised locally, plus a committee already assembled and eager to take on the world, by all accounts.

But what tickled my fancy most was his description of the church and its setting: *Nestled among fourteen acres of native woodland, St. Sannan's Church has sat derelict and unattended for a quarter century. We, the committee and parishioners of Bilbury, are eager to see it restored to its former glory.*

And the description of the stained-glass window had me chomping at the bit…

The window is situated in the apse, at the far end of the chancel. It faces the altar and is approximately seven feet tall and three feet wide. A magnificent specimen in its heyday, I imagine, though now sadly bereft of almost all its glass sections.

When I read those words, my heart had sunk, imagining having to replace antique glass with modern, but he had gone on to say that a number of sections had been found among the rubble, and he believed that more lay hidden within the building and grounds. The description appealed to the child in me. Finding the missing pieces would be like playing a game of hide and seek.

As a student I studied the art and history of stained glass, but so far I have not been lucky enough to restore such a grand specimen. My studio work tends towards the commercial side of things: bespoke designs, both modern and traditional, for homes and offices, and the odd vintage restoration job, but nothing as exciting as this. My heart lies in antique glass, Victorian Gothic and authentic art deco in particular, but opportunities to restore either are rare.

My guess is the church window originates from the nineteenth century, a period that saw a revival in religious iconographic stained glass, often copied directly from famous oil paintings. What a joy it would be to restore, and in a remote setting, too. An opportunity to exchange the noise of traffic and the smell of exhaust fumes for the wind in the trees and the fresh air, at least for a couple of weeks.

THE GPS IS as confused as I am and sends me round and round in circles. The chocolate-box town of Bilbury, a mere twenty miles from home, proved easy to find, though having only lived in the county for seven months I'm not familiar with it. The trouble is, after passing through the township, I cannot find my bearings. The location of the church remains a mystery.

Having checked its whereabouts on Google Maps before setting off, I have some idea of its general location, because although the church itself was not visible on the satellite view, the surrounding woods were. A glance at the clock informs me I'm already five minutes late. I *hate* being late. "*If you're early, you're on time. If you're on time, you're late,*" my father used to say when I was growing up. He was a stickler for all sorts of things, most of which did more harm than good.

Whichever way I turn, I end up driving my van along narrow lanes banked high on both sides, the kind of lanes you drive with your heart in your mouth in case a tractor's coming in the opposite direction. I regret not having obtained a mobile number from Mr. Hargreaves, though I doubt there's a signal here in any case.

A nagging doubt enters my mind. What if I'm driving into a trap? This self-labeled *chairman* might be a crook, one who arranges to meet a woman at a remote location under the pretense of offering them their dream job, while beneath the cloak he is nothing more than a wolf. Come to think of it, why would a committee choose such a remote location for a community center and make people drive miles to get there? They're usually located within town centers to be accessible to the local population.

In accepting his offer to meet and view the proposed restoration, I had signed the letter Ms Robin Griffiths, thereby establishing my gender. Yes, he had assumed me to be male in his initial correspondence, though what the hell difference would it make if he were some kind of maniac?

If I were to disappear, the police would find no evidence. No contact number on my mobile; no agreed meet-up on my website form. *Get a grip, Robin, for god's sake!*

I pull in beside a farm gate and take a few deep breaths to calm my nerves. My palms are slick with sweat, as is my top lip. Perhaps I should abandon the mission. Go home and remain in blissful ignorance of what might have been.

A curious lamb wanders from its mother and stands at the gate, watching me. It bleats a word of encouragement before its mother calls it back. The newborn lambs in the field beyond the gate look so innocent in their white coats that the world suddenly feels less threatening. I'll drive for a minute longer, I tell myself, and if I can't find it, I'll turn around and head for home. I pull away from the grassy verge and head downhill.

Rounding a bend, I spy in the distance what I assume is Coppersgate Woods, since it's the only woods I've noticed since leaving town. *Take a sharp left, then bear right*, Hargreaves' confirmation letter had said. *You'll see a dirt track through the woods. After half a mile or so, the church will be on your left. There's no car park as such, but you can park in front of the gate.*

My stomach does another somersault. Am I being baited? Still, I'm here now, and the road's too narrow to turn around, so I have no choice but to continue.

The track is rutted, and although my attention is focused more on the potholes than my surroundings, I see enough to suggest this woods is broadleaf rather than conifer. The trees are newly budded and peppered with birdsong; the air is tainted with wild garlic.

I spot his car in the distance, parked in front of a stone wall: a silver Peugeot 108 that looks too small to hide a body in, unless he dissected it first.

He must have heard the rumble of my wheels, as he appears at the gate. He's wearing a crumpled linen suit and a khaki cotton hat more suited to an Australian summer than a British spring. He is older than I imagined, around the age of seventy, I guess. Instinct suggests all is well, especially when he offers a friendly wave. I've learned to trust my instinct over the years, after everything I've been through.

I park beneath the overhanging bough of a yew, one whose roots have burst through a section of stone wall, causing it to crumble. I turn off the engine and step out of the van.

"Ah, you found us at last," he says, wearing an innocuous smile and dark glasses—the purple-mirrored kind worn by aging rock-stars—which clashes with the rest of his image. "Take some navigating, these roads."

"Sorry I'm late." My face burns red, and when he holds out a hand for me to shake, I swipe my palm down the front of my jeans before doing so. His hand is cool in contrast to mine.

"Never mind, never mind. You made it and that's all that matters. Jonathan Hargreaves, pleased to meet you."

"Robin Griffiths." I manage to return the smile.

He gestures towards the churchyard. "Come on in, but be warned: it's rather dilapidated."

At the lychgate he pauses and points towards a tangle of bramble that has woven itself around the wood. "Careful here. It's the reason I wear a hat whenever I come. Damn thorns will scratch your eyes out good as look at you." He shoulders his way through the gate and holds back a long shoot to allow me to enter. "I've arranged for someone to cut it back at the end of the week. We need to clear the access if we want you builders to be able to do your job."

I can hardly be termed a builder, but I let the comment slide.

The stress of the last few minutes turns to awe as I step through the gate into the graveyard.

Ahead stands the church, an ancient Cotswold-stone building complete with narthex and bell tower, but it is the graveyard itself that steals my breath. Scattered headstones peep from behind knee-high grass, some of the stones leaning towards each other as if conspiring. The wind whispers through the trees, giving them a voice: *visitors, visitors!*

"Some of these trees will need to be felled," he says, startling me from my reverie. "Over the years, nature has done what she does best, and, as you can see, the woodland trees have seeded themselves among the graves."

He's right, of course. Here and there, headstones lie toppled by saplings that have matured into full-grown trees, their roots desecrating what should have been someone's place of eternal rest. I picture bones and roots intertwined. A ribcage through which fibrous strands have woven a web strong enough to pin down the skeleton, ensuring it remains in situ for eternity.

"Anyway, the window," he says. "Walk this way."

A mossy path littered with pine cones and bird shit leads towards the church and then around the back to the chancel. The windows along the longitudinal wall are diamond-leaded with plain glass, most of which is broken or cracked, despite having been covered in heavy-duty mesh. I imagine he will want me to repair these, too, though he hasn't mentioned it yet. A gust of wind screams in my face as we round the corner, forcing me to stand still for a moment and wait for its tantrum to fizzle out.

"And here we have it," he says, pointing at the window.

I crane my neck to gain a better view but need to take a few steps back onto the grass to see it properly. The stone sill stands at chest height and the window rises from there, reaching a height of approximately twelve feet. On either side of it are lancet windows, elongated eyes that reinforce the sensation of the structure pointing skywards.

Unlike the other windows, the stained-glass window – if that's what it can be called, for now only a few determined pieces remain captive within its leaded frame – has no mesh to protect it. Clinging to the wall is a tangle of ivy that reaches long tendrils in heaven's direction.

I gaze up at the shattered window. It must have been spectacular in its day, but now it is impossible to tell what biblical scene it once depicted. Broken things have always piqued my interest, people included: the ruined, the desecrated, those who have been violated, lure me in, hook, line and sinker.

"What do you think?"

I squint towards the window, hands on hips. "It must have been impressive once. Perhaps there's some kind of record—a photograph or something—from when the church was in use?"

He frowns. "There are none. Trust me, I've looked. I'm the first to admit I'm no dab-hand when it comes to computers, but my secretary is pretty tech-minded, and she's been unable to find anything. Not a single photograph anywhere."

"How strange... and the locals? Surely someone must have attended the church in the past. I mean, if it's only been closed for twenty-five years or so, someone must remember it."

He pinches his lower lip between thumb and forefinger, a habit, perhaps. "You'd think so, wouldn't you? Most folk attended the church in town rather than this one. I guess the place is too remote."

I say nothing, certain he must be mistaken. Surely the church would have had a caretaker at the very least. I'll do some research myself. And, if I find nothing, at least I'll have the leadwork to go by. Determining which colors to use will be nigh on impossible without a photo though. "In your letter, you mentioned you found some of the glass. Is it possible for me to see it? It'll give me an idea of the window's age."

"Of course. It's inside the church." He turns as if to walk away, then stops. "Actually, you might get a better impression of the window itself from inside. At least the sun won't be in your eyes."

He marches ahead, and I follow like a lamb along the narrow path. "So, my guess is the parish council now own the church. Is that right?"

"Indeed," he says over his shoulder, "and we bought it for a snip of a price. Though once we're inside, you'll see the reason for that. The place needs so much work."

Back at the main entrance, a sturdy wooden door bars the way. Four straps of rusted metal bolster its strength, and a ring of iron attached to an intricately carved backplate serves as a handle. It is unlocked; he must have opened it while waiting for me to arrive. The door yields with no more than a plaintive creak and opens into a narthex and beyond to the nave.

What strikes me first is the biting cold. I'd expected the spring sunshine to have thawed its old shell a little, but this is not the case. Each breath I exhale emits a small cloud, and I clench my teeth to prevent them from chattering. It must be close to zero in here.

A flutter of wings spooks me, but it is just a wood pigeon startled from the rafters by our sudden appearance. I turn my eyes skyward, noting that half the roof tiles are missing. The building is crowned by a wooden skeleton, with nothing more than a tangled wig of ivy and the leafy limb of an encroaching yew to protect it from the elements. Little wonder it's so cold and damp.

He points at the missing portion of roof. "See what I mean? There's an awful lot of work to do, but it'll be worth it in the end, I'm sure."

I admire his tenacity. The place is a wreck. Far worse than I realized from the outside.

The wood pigeon returns to its barren nest on the rafter, from where it eyes us suspiciously, occasionally cooing its disapproval.

Leaning against a stone pillar, I take in my surroundings. Where door meets lintel, a lace-web spider stops work and watches from the heart of its cunning web. Wrapped in a silk shroud, an insect awaits its fate. I hope it's already dead.

I cast my gaze around the interior. A central aisle and Gothic arches. The place is imposing, but my god, what a state of ruin! Broken roof tiles lie scattered on pews so thick with dust I could write my name in the dirt.

"Geez, you're not kidding. Has it been vandalized, or are the elements to blame?"

"No idea, I'm afraid. Now then… the pieces of glass." He dashes down the aisle, and I follow.

A substantial stone altar sits in front of the apse a few feet in front of the broken window. On first appearance, it looks as if the altar is strewn with litter and debris, but on closer inspection I realize it is not litter but the skeletons of leaves and desiccated flowers. They cover its pitted surface, their once vibrant colors faded to sepia. I pick up a leaf and it crumbles to dust between my fingers. *Ashes to ashes, dust to dust.*

Hargreaves' voice brings me back to the present. "Here." He opens the lid of a crude wooden box. "These are the pieces we've found so far."

I select a shard and hold it toward the light streaking in through the broken window. Oxblood red, roughly crescent shaped, like a miniature spleen. I know in an instant that it's old because of its opalescence. I hold it in the palm of my hand. "Post 1880, I think."

He studies me, expecting more.

I point at the window. "My initial guess would be that it was made between 1880 and 1910, art nouveau rather than art deco."

"And you know this how?" His tone implies interest rather than skepticism.

"Because of the long curving lines. If it were art deco, the lines would be more geometric, more angular."

He rubs his chin and nods.

"Strange how the leadwork's intact. It's as if someone

came along and popped the pieces of glass out with a thumb, though I imagine once I'm able to examine the leadwork it'll be soft. If that's the case, it'll need replacing."

"Hmm…Well, you have my permission to do whatever it takes. By the way, we've hired a contractor that works specifically in the conservation of old buildings such as this. Hywel Elliot & Co. You might have heard of them."

"I'm afraid I haven't. I moved to this area quite recently. Still finding my way around."

"They cover all aspects of building work except stained-glass repair, which is why I contacted you." He pauses. "So, how do you feel now that you've seen the place?"

I turn to face him and my distorted reflection stares back at me in the mirrored lenses of his glasses. Despite the distortion, my expression looks eager. "I'm definitely interested, but I'll need a hand to take out the window, and I'll require scaffolding because of its height. Once the window's removed, I'll be able to work here inside the church for much of the renovation." In truth, it would be easier to have the window transported back to the studio, but a few weeks' work in such magnificent surroundings is just what I could do with right now. As long as I bring everything I need, I can set up a workshop of sorts here. And besides, it might be nice to have a bit of company. If other conservation work is going on at the same time, I'll get to meet new people. Plus, there'll be others to hand to help me replace the window once it's restored.

Eyeing the space between the altar and broken window, I picture the scene. Three or four trestles with plenty of space to maneuverer from all four sides.

He sees me pondering. "I forgot to mention in my letter that the other windows will need repairing too. Are you willing to see to all of them?"

"Of course. They'll be much simpler to repair with the plain glass."

He claps his hands, then rubs them together. "Rightio. Will you send me an estimate of costs, or is it too soon?"

"I'm afraid I'll have to see what we're up against once the window's removed. It will depend on how much leadwork needs replacing, and on whether the remaining pieces of glass can be found."

"Of course. I understand."

I replace the oxblood shard in the box and close the lid. "Do you mind if I take this home? I'd like to dig a little deeper, if that's okay. And I'll take a few photos of the window before I leave, for research purposes."

"Not at all. Do as you wish."

I whip out my phone and take some photos while he waits. "How soon can you start?"

I make a quick mental calculation, considering the job I'm in the middle of. "How does a week Monday sound?"

"Grand. The builders are due to start work at the end of this week, so anytime after that will be fine. I'll give you a spare set of keys. Then you can come and go as you please."

I lift the box of glass, which is substantial in weight, and tuck it under my arm, eager to return to the warmth of the van. "Is there electricity here?"

"There is, but I'm not keen on it being used until it's been certified. The builders have been asked to prioritize that. They need electricity to operate their tools, so I'm certain they'll see to it quickly. By the time you start work, it should be sorted."

I make a mental note to bring a small heater with me and follow him down the aisle.

"Would it be okay if I pop back in my spare time to look for more missing pieces of glass? I rather fancy a scout around." I rub my forearms, trying to warm them. "I'll remember to wear a coat next time. It's freezing in here."

"Of course, though I might as well tell you… most of the glass was found outside among the gravestones, not inside."

We step into the relative warmth of an April day, and he frowns. "It's strange. You'd swear they'd been scattered to the wind by some giant hand."

"Pardon?"

"The pieces of glass." He makes a wide sweep with his arm. "Here, there, everywhere."

The thought of someone intentionally scattering the glass makes me flinch. Why would anyone do such a thing? "I wonder, do you have a mobile number I could contact you on?"

He snorts. "What, those modern fandangled things? I refuse to own one. Hate everything they stand for. But I'll give you the telephone number of my secretary's office in case of emergencies. Do you have a pen?"

I pull out my mobile and grin. "It's okay, I'll store it on this." However, having added his number, I want to give him mine as well. I check my van and find a pen. No paper though, so I scribble my mobile number on the back of a chewing-gum wrapper and hand it to him. "Here… in case you need to contact me."

"One moment," he says, opening his car door. He rummages about in the glove compartment. "Here." He hands me a bunch of keys. "Feel free to return whenever you like."

TWO

BACK HOME, I boot the laptop and transfer the photos of the window from my phone, preferring to view them on a larger screen. The first photo I open is blurred, so I skip to the next, and the next, frustrated to find all of them blurred. I check the images on the phone and discover the same. Either the camera is broken, or there was insufficient light in the church, and I forgot to use the flash. Damn! I'd taken them in a hurry because I'd been concerned about keeping Hargreaves waiting.

I reload the first image to see if anything can be salvaged from it. If not, I'll have to go back soon and take some more, because I'm eager to discover what image the window represents. I zoom in, examining one section at a time. The photo is not so much blurred as just indistinct—hazy, as though faded by decades of sunshine.

But when I zoom back out, the image looks different to how it did previously. Now the photo suggests the window is more complete than it was in reality. This is crazy! Nevertheless, the window appears whole again. No evidence of missing glass; instead, it depicts a riot of faded color. If my mind is not playing tricks, a figure dominates the center of the image. Featureless, yet donned in a cobalt and oxblood cloak. A saint of some kind, I assume. Most likely Saint Sannan, the church's namesake.

I search the name of the church online, hoping to discover an image that matches this one, but the search leads me to two churches in Wales: one in the north and another in the south. I can find no mention of a church named St. Sannan's in this part of England. The church in South Wales has a stained-glass window, but the saint depicted is robed in green, not red and blue.

I return my screen to the zoomed-in photo and open the wooden box containing the shards of glass. I select the kidney-shaped piece and hold it up against the image on the screen. A definite color match, though the on-screen version is muted.

I rummage around in the box until I find a blue shard and hold it up to the image. Again, an exact match. How is this possible?

The urge to drive straight back to the church is powerful, but a glance out the window tells me the daylight is already dimming. I have a job to complete tomorrow but should finish by around two if I skip lunch, then I can return to the church. One thing I know for certain: the window was missing almost all of its glass. So what I'm seeing here must be a trick of the light. Either that or there's something wrong with my phone camera. I'll take my SLR tomorrow, just in case.

My stomach rumbles, reminding me I haven't eaten since breakfast. A sandwich will suffice. I can eat at the computer.

I spend the next two hours searching for information on the church's history and discover nothing whatsoever. No entry exists on the National Church Trust database, nothing on any of the historical sites. The church doesn't even get a mention on local sites. It feels as though today's meeting with Jonathan Hargreaves was no more than a figment of my imagination. How is it possible for a building to stand for eight-hundred years yet leave no trace?

I guess the answer is simple: either I misread the name on Hargreaves' letter or he wrote the wrong name.

I slide open the desk drawer, retrieve the letter, and scan the text. No, I was not mistaken, he definitely called it *St. Sannan's*. He must have made an error.

But then I remember him mentioning that neither he nor his secretary could find any records. Is it possible there are none?

It makes no sense. This is the twenty-first century, goddammit, it should be easy to find something online. There must be public records of the deeds transfer. If Bilbury Parish Council purchased the church, then who did they purchase it from?

A sense of dread seeps into the room. What if the whole thing's a scam? What if there is no church-restoration company, and I spend several weeks working on a project for which I won't get paid? I try to recall the name of the conservation company Hargreaves mentioned but draw a blank. A Google search throws up a list of a few, and I scan the names. There… third result down: Hywel Elliot & Co. I'm certain it was it.

I could call them on some pretense or other to check they've been assigned the job, but what excuse would I give? They might consider such information private.

I sit, chin cupped in hands, and stare at the screen. The counselor's words ring clear in my ears, so close they tickle. *You have to learn to trust, Robin, or life will continue to be difficult.* I know she's right, but it's easier said than done, especially when you're damaged goods.

I picture Jonathan Hargreaves with his honest smile and firm handshake. His granddad hat to protect him from the bramble. What kind of scammer wears a hat like that?

Gut instinct suggests nothing's amiss, but there's a part of me that refuses to let go of the old fears. After all, no one seemed more convincing than my own father. No one. Everyone loved and admired him. Capable of charming the birds off the trees. The definition of altruism. A more benevolent and God-fearing man you couldn't wish to meet, at least on the surface. Only I saw through the veneer. Even my mother saw no wrong in him, though I prefer to think she did but was too afraid to admit it. A classic *enabler*, my counselor called her, and I guess she was right. Every narcissist needs at least one enabler in their life, and my mother fit the role to perfection. He also had my sister, *the golden child* who could do no wrong. And then there was me, *the scapegoat*.

Yes, each of us fit our roles seamlessly. It took me twenty-two years to realize what those roles entailed and to try to come to terms with the verdict. The family that seemed so perfect was less so once you peeled back the layers.

Trust. I think back to the final conversation I had with my mother, the day I was brave enough to cut the ties for good. Like a portioned cake, the slices could never be put back together again. Not without the jam bleeding into the cream.

Enough dwelling on the past. What I need now is distraction, so—instead of focusing on how the whole thing is a setup—I spread the glass segments out on the desk and turn my attention to researching and recording their attributes.

My instinct was correct: the evidence suggests the glass dates from the late-nineteenth century or thereabouts, though the shape of the window dates back to much earlier: Gothic in style with a pointed arch, typical of the period. Once I'm able to take a closer look and inspect the leadwork and beveling, I can be more accurate. And if I were to discover more information about the building,

I might be able to find the name of the original artist, which would be wonderful.

I refuse to surrender. I'll visit Bilbury Library to carry out some research and make an appointment to meet someone from the local council if necessary. The window has sharpened its claws and refuses to let go.

THREE

I STEP INTO the street outside my studio, and a chilly breeze whips my hair across my eyes, momentarily blinding me from the traffic. I tuck it behind my ears and wait for the lights to change before dashing across and heading for the bakery.

I'd been in the studio by seven and worked through lunch so I could finish early. The studio, no bigger than a garage, is a little rental just off the High Street and only a hundred yards or so from my bedsit. My father would not approve of either the location or my choice of career, but it's none of his business, and since I no longer have anything to do with him it doesn't matter.

Control, that was what my father wanted. Both my parents had pushed me towards the sciences, in which I had no interest—and as for maths, let's not go there. Because I refused to comply with their wishes, they refused to help fund my university degree. Out of sheer determination to seek a career in history and the arts, I worked two part-time jobs and funded my own education, managing to get by with a small student loan at the end because of my frugality.

Narcissism isn't just about appearance and vanity—it goes far deeper than that—and his refusal to help had nothing to do with my choice of subjects; it was all about that control. My parents were quite well-off—my dad working as a senior civil service manager and my mother a teacher—but they used their wealth as a tool to drive a wedge between me and my sister, Wren. It worked when we were children. If there was a specific toy I longed to have for Christmas, they bought it for her instead; but the older I got, the more I saw through their ploy and the less I fell for it. I became adept at hiding my true feelings, thus denying them their craving for control. So what if Wren has never bought her own car. So what if she owns a plush pad without a mortgage. I'll not be bought like she has.

Pastry in hand, I set off for the church.

As I round the final bend, Coppersgate Woods comes into view, the freshly leaved canopy of trees bursting with spring pride. The van rumbles along the dirt track leading to the church, its tires the only sound for miles, and yet, as I park outside the church, I feel as if I am being watched.

It does not take long for me to spot the culprit. As I exit the van and slam the door, a crow issues a throaty *caw*. It sits high in the overgrown yew, its claws hooked and tail fanned. Its expression is solemn, and for some strange reason reminds me of my grandmother.

Its beady eyes follow me as I open the gate, remembering to hold back the spiny stems of bramble with the sleeve of my coat. Before passing through, I check to see if I have missed a billboard announcing the name of the church, but there is none.

The back of my neck prickles as I recall the words my grandmother spoke the first time she took me to visit Pappi's grave: *Yew trees thrive on corpses, Robin. The dead provide good nutrients. The tree will feed on them, and a new yew will spring forth from the old. That's why they're the symbol of death and rebirth.* I guess I inherited my imagination from my grandmother, because neither of my parents have a creative bone in their body.

The way in which the sunken headstones lean towards one another, combined with the whispering long grass, once again gives me the sense of the dead conspiring. I tell myself not to be ridiculous and pick my way along the path towards the door.

I retrieve the keys from my coat pocket, select the largest, and insert it into the lock. The backplate is intricately carved, but the metal is too pitted and oxidized for me to make out the pattern clearly. I peer closely and can just make out some kind of scrolled foliage with the outline of a figure at the center, around which the foliage weaves a path, disguising the figure from prying eyes.

I look for the name of the church inside the narthex, but again there is none. On entering the nave, I am greeted by a cold blast of air, and the old wood pigeon takes flight in a frenzied flutter. The sound of its beating wings startles me, just as it did the first time.

Sunlight pours in through the once-stained-glass window, extending a long-armed beam down the aisle. Breathtaking! But I am here for the purpose of research, not to get carried away by the atmosphere of this derelict place. I check the walls close to the entrance, in search of the church's name. Nothing but flaking paint and spider webs.

No evidence of the church's name anywhere. Jonathan Hargreaves could have called it anything, and I'd be none the wiser. Perhaps this is why I can find no trace online.

Once again, my sixth sense issues a word of warning. *Tread carefully*, it says. *All is not what it seems.*

I cast my gaze around the whole interior, taking in the Gothic arches that straddle the aisle, the steeply pitched roof, and the chancel that runs east to west at the furthest end. A musty smell hangs in the air, tickling my nose. I sneeze, and the sound echoes all around, emphasizing how alone I am.

The building has been stripped of all artifacts and furniture, apart from a few rotten pews and the stone altar. No wall-mounted memorials, candlesticks, crucifixes, or any religious paraphernalia remain. The altar, which sits at the top of two steps in the chancel, was far too heavy for anyone to remove, I imagine. Is this how the committee inherited the church, or have they stripped it of its artifacts in preparation for renovation?

I concede defeat in my mission to discover the church's name and turn my attention to the stained-glass window. Because much of the leadwork remains, from this distance it is possible to gain an impression of the overall window. As the photos had revealed, the design suggests that a figure once resided within the center. A vague outline of a head and shoulders remains, but that's all. But the computer screen had shown color, too. I'm certain. The previous evening feels like a dream. A warped sense of reality, my mind over-fatigued and therefore open to imagining all kinds of scenarios.

My father had always belittled me for what he termed *prone to embellishing the facts*. He used it as a way of making me doubt myself and to suggest I was lying, whereas he, of course, was nothing but honest.

My mother, the dutiful enabler, reinforced his opinion of me on so many occasions that I came to believe it. Only when I was knee-deep in therapy did I begin to think differently.

I walk the length of the aisle, up the chancel steps, and stand in front of the window, straining my neck to study its full height. At the thought of what this will take to renovate, my fists clench from both self-doubt and excitement. If only I had an image to work from. I have no intention of giving up on that hope yet. Perhaps the library in Bilbury will offer something in the way of records.

I raise my hand and imagine drawing a line, sectioning off the bottom six or seven inches with an invisible divider. Then I use the leaded outline to count the missing pieces of glass from that section. Twenty-two. Given that the window is seven feet tall, the total must be around three hundred pieces. The box Jonathan Hargreaves gave me contained fifty-five. My heart sinks. The box contains a trifling number of pieces compared to the total number. What on earth have I let myself in for? The urge to run from the building and never return overwhelms me, but at that moment the sunlight highlights a twinkling sliver of glass trapped between wall and skirting board.

I remove the camera from around my neck, place it on the altar, then kneel on the stone-cold floor and try to pluck the piece out with my thumb and forefinger. Not enough of the glass protrudes, and I fail to grip it. It reminds me of long ago when a sliver of glass from a jam jar had buried itself in my finger as I twisted the lid. The tiny sliver had refused to budge, though it eventually worked its way out of its own accord, my body rejecting the foreign object.

I pull the keys from my pocket, select the smallest, and insert it into the narrow gap between wall and skirting. However, rather than helping to lever the slither out, the key jams. I jiggle the key about until eventually it springs free, but not without having pushed the shard of glass deeper into the groove. I groan with frustration. Finding one more piece of glass is a spit in the ocean, but I can be obsessive, and I refuse to relinquish possession of the piece.

I get to my feet and look around for something sharp to use as a lever. In the far corner of the chancel, I find a nail: an old-fashioned type with a hand-forged head and burred shank, but to me it's a gift of gold.

My heart pounds as I slot the nail into the gap, fearing it might push the shard in deeper just as the key did. I wipe the sweat from my palm on my coat so I can grip it properly. I'm aware of the sound of my own breathing but of something else, too. The breath of another. Again, the sense of being watched is real, and I raise my head to look around before I can focus on the task in hand. Needless to say, there's no one here.

At last, I manage to dig the nail in deep enough and hook it underneath the piece of glass. Little by little, I prise it from its hiding place until enough of it is exposed for me to grip with my fingers. The sense of satisfaction as the piece reveals itself is immense. Approximately three inches by two, the shard is roughly rectangular with rounded corners, and the color of good cognac with a hint of smoke. Another old piece, for sure. I slip it into my pocket for safekeeping and then shuffle the length of skirting on my knees, searching for any other pieces lodged there, but I am disappointed to find none.

Reminding myself that the main purpose of today's visit is to take photographs, I retrieve the SLR from the altar and take some pictures of the window, taking care to ensure the flash is on.

Shivering with cold, I wander outside and take a few external photos. At least the sun is behind me, which I'm grateful for, since I've forgotten to bring the lens hood.

While I'm outside, I scout around to see if I can find any pieces of glass near the window. I focus my search on the ivy that clings to the wall, hoping a shard might have got caught among the leaves. I trail the vines with my finger. Is the ivy poisonous? I might develop a rash later as my skin is particularly sensitive. Despite the risk, I cannot resist digging deeper into the tangled vines, and my efforts are rewarded when I find two more pieces: one blue, the other rust-red, like a bloodstain that's been left too long.

On the ground, jutting a centimeter or so above the dirt, is what looks like a third piece. I dig about with the toe of my shoe. There—it's cobalt blue but caked in mud. I kneel on the damp grass, flicking my beige coat out of the way to keep it clean, and scrape the dirt with my fingers. They come away soiled but bearing a gift. I spit on a corner and rub at the glass with a tissue, revealing a shard the color of a dunnock's egg.

Finding the pieces has turned into an Easter egg hunt; the thrill of discovering each shard provides a tiny dopamine fix and incites a lust for more. The thought sparks a memory of my father berating me for eating too many chocolate eggs. His voice rings loud in my head: *You'll make yourself sick, Robin; and besides, you'll get fat. You're already too plump around the middle, if you want my opinion.*

I did not want his opinion. I had never wanted his opinion, though he gave it often enough. God forbid I should put on weight and destroy his image of the perfect little family. I mean, what would people think if he had a fat daughter? The memory is sobering, and I am suddenly deflated.

I've done what I came here to do, so I decide to call it a day and head for home. There's always tomorrow. Shoulders hunched, I skulk around to the front of the church and along the path, but halfway to the van I remember the church door is still unlocked. I head back to the main door to secure the church. The rusty lock squeals in protest as if it does not wish to be held captive.

As I approach the gate, the call of the crow sends a shiver down my spine. It stands on guard, perched on the left gatepost and eyeing me with black-beaded pupils and pure-white irises. An old crow then, not a juvenile. Perhaps it thinks it owns the place and sees me as an intruder.

I draw close, and it refuses to move, though it hops from foot to foot as if it cannot bear its own weight for long.

I shouldn't be afraid of the frail old thing. "Shoo!" I say and push the gate open. It squeals on its hinges. Still, the crow does not move. It hops forward and issues a loud *craa!* that makes me cower.

I hurry through the gate, shoot the lock, and jump into my van, slinging my bag onto the passenger seat. As I pull away from the church, the bag gapes open, revealing my camera. I hope and pray that today's photos will prove more successful than those I took previously. The sun reads my thoughts and winks at the camera lens, temporarily blinding me.

FOUR

A SENSE OF unease accompanies me on the journey home. Something feels off, though I cannot pinpoint it. As I approach the picturesque town of Bilbury, I glance at the clock: 16:32. Will I have time to call at the library before it closes for the day? Trouble is, I don't know where the library is, or if one even exists.

Bilbury is such a pretty town, honey-colored with quintessential English charm, though not the easiest to navigate due to the narrow road that runs through the middle. I turn left and follow the sign to the car park, convincing myself I need a few basic provisions in any case, so it will not be a waste of time.

The map on the billboard at the car-park entrance assures me there is a library just off High Street in Stitches Lane. What a fabulous street name. No doubt it was connected with a haberdashery or drapers in times past.

I park the van and wander along the High Street in the direction of Stitches Lane. This late in the day, the town is as sleepy as a pollen-laden bee, and I soon find myself in a narrow, cobbled street, unsuitable for vehicles. The sense of having slipped back in time is acute.

Stitches Lane, a sign on the wall says. The library stands halfway along in a picture-book building of yellow Cotswold stone. I climb the three steps to the entrance and find myself in a world scented with old books and floor polish.

The wooden countertop is chest height, so tall I can barely see the librarian who sits in front of a computer screen on the other side, tapping away at the keys. She glances at the clock as I approach and offers a weak smile. "Afternoon," she says. "Can I help?"

"I wonder…Do you have any information on St. Sannan's?"

Her left eye twitches, and she looks me up and down before turning her attention back to the computer screen. She doesn't reply, so I ask again. "The church in Coppersgate Woods. The derelict building?"

She looks at the clock on the wall and sighs. "There might be something in the local history section, but I'm afraid we're about to close."

I shuffle my feet. "Okay, I'll come back another time."

She nods, then resumes typing, cutting me dead.

As I'm walking away, invisible fingers tap me on the shoulder and a voice whispers in my ear: *Hey, don't allow her to bully you!*

"You know what," I say, glancing at the clock. "I think I'll take a quick look before you close."

Her face is as fiery as her hair. She points over her shoulder with her thumb. "First bookcase on the left. I believe there's something on local churches."

A surge of triumph accompanies my racing heart. My counselor taught me self-assertion techniques, but opportunities to put them into practice are rare.

The librarian's eyes bore into my back as I search the shelf, but she offers no help. Nevertheless, I soon locate a promising title: *Bilbury: Places of Worship*, by G. Moniker. The book is more of a pamphlet, just thirty or so pages printed on glossy paper.

I flick through, noting the black-and-white photographs. My guess is it's old, out of print most likely. I flip back to the copyright page: first published in 1974. I skip to the index and skim for the words St. Sannan's. Success! A church by that name is listed on page twelve.

The page shows a black-and-white photograph of the church, undoubtedly the one I just left, albeit in a better state of repair. The woods are less mature, less impinging on the building than they are now. Beneath it are the words: *St. Sannan's, Coppersgate Woods, formerly known as—*

The original name of the church has been blotted out with Tippex. How frustrating! Why on earth would someone do such a thing?

A brief paragraph states: "*Little is known of the history of St. Sannan's, in all likelihood due to its remote location. It is believed to originate from the thirteenth century but has been subject to many alterations over time.*"

And that's it.

Such a disappointment. Ah well, at least I've confirmed the current name of the place.

I take the pamphlet over to the counter, where the librarian is already donning her coat.

"May I borrow this, please?"

She scratches the side of her nose with a brightly painted fingernail. "Yes, but you'll have to come back tomorrow. I've just turned the computer off."

"Then can you keep it behind the desk for me?" I hold the pamphlet out and she takes it from me and places it on a shelf below the counter where I can no longer see it. "Thank you," I say, the words brittle as ice.

It's not until I'm a mile or so from Bilbury that I realize I forgot to buy bread and milk. In fact, the little town had been a blur after the library incident.

BACK HOME, I heat a can of soup and butter some bread and then power my laptop, eager to transfer the photos from the SLR. The tightness in my chest eases as I open the first photo, one taken from inside the church. There is no blurring and nothing strange about the photograph: it's just a broken window with missing glass. I skip through the rest, pleased to find nothing amiss. My phone camera must have been to blame for the hazy faded color and featureless figure.

I spend a considerable amount of time looking through the photos, zooming in and out to examine the leadwork that outlines the figure at the center. With so many pieces missing it's impossible to gain more than the impression of a figure garbed in red and blue. I will need to be patient if I'm going to solve the puzzle of how this once looked. *Good things come to those who wait, Robin.* My father's words are never far away.

The third photo was taken from the apse at a slight angle, because the stone altar was too close for me to fit in the whole window. There, in the bottom right-hand corner, is a shadow. I look closer, and my heart skips a beat. The shadow is roughly human-shaped, though elongated, as are most shadows during late afternoon. It looks as if someone was standing just behind me, casting a shadow on the wall and floor. It has to be a trick of the light, doesn't it? I recall the feeling of being watched, and shiver.

I check through the other photos and find nothing else unusual, so I power down the computer and am about to get ready for bed when I remember the pieces of glass I found earlier. My coat remains on the sofa where I threw it, my mother's voice in my head reprimanding me for being untidy. My parents were fastidious in every way, and it's been tough to adapt to living in a more relaxed fashion.

I dig through the pocket, pull out the pieces of glass, and

throw the coat back on the sofa. "There you go, Mum," I whisper. "My home, and I'll do what I want."

I fill the bathroom basin with hot soapy water and slide in the three pieces of glass from my pocket and the slivers from the box Jonathan Hargreaves gave me. Then, I clean each section with a washcloth. Several are caked with dirt, and I have to replace the water in the sink a few times.

Once they're clean, I lay them on top of an old white towel in the bath to air-dry. Fifty-eight sections in total. It will take a miracle for me to find enough shards to make a difference, which is such a shame. Modern glass is not the same, but antique glass is so expensive. Nevertheless, the decision is Hargreaves' to make, not mine. He might consider it a worthwhile investment.

I pick out one of the oxblood pieces and hold it towards the light. Striations of deep red, like a good Merlot, swirl from top to bottom, and there are striations of rust too, more towards the brown palette. As I lean forward to replace it on the towel, the wet shard slips from my grasp. I make a grab for it and feel a sharp pain. A cut across the tip of my index finger, approximately a centimeter in length, from which a scarlet rivulet runs.

I rinse the wound in cold water, grateful the shard was clean, then dry my hand. The blood refuses to stop until I find a Band-Aid to wrap round it. Feeling a little shaky, I switch off the light and head for bed without bothering to shower.

IN THE EARLY hours of the morning, I wake with a raging thirst and sore throat. I drag myself into the bathroom, realizing I must have forgotten to draw the blind. Moonlight creeps in at the window, highlighting the shards of glass spread in the bath. They twinkle as I pass by. Alive. I switch on the light, extinguishing both stars and twinkling glass.

I swallow two paracetamols, flinching with the pain. I can't afford to be ill now, not with two jobs to finish working on before I can concentrate on the church. But my cheeks burn hot, and I feel a bit shaky. A virus, most likely. All I can do is hope that the pills kick in and that I feel better in the morning.

FIVE

BETWEEN TRYING TO wrap up a few jobs, and battling sickness, I am unable to revisit the church until Saturday. The cut on my finger hasn't helped. Swollen and oozing pus, it not only made glass cutting and soldering difficult but it also made me feverish. A constant headache and nausea so acute I began to wonder if there might be a more sinister cause—tetanus perhaps, or worse still, anthrax. Then last night, I removed the dressing to see that the cut had healed, as if by magic. It had taken the nausea with it and left behind no more than an angry scar.

The first thing I notice when I arrive is that the bramble has been cut back. The lychgate is free of its spiny thorns and is far more welcoming. The old yew has been given a haircut too, though I doubt the crow is happy about it. It's absent today—off sulking no doubt.

The grass has also been cut. No whispering foliage announces my arrival, and the air is heavy and scented with petrichor following last night's rain. Without the long grass to disguise them, the headstones appear more alert, as if they have woken from a long sleep. A cluster stands beneath the boughs of the yew, two of them butting up against one another, leaning shoulder to shoulder for comfort. The stone on the left has sunk into the earth and is shorter than the other. They look like a parent and child. Both are green with lichen, but the shorter of the two wears a braid of ivy. I take a closer look, but neither are marked with decipherable words. The inscription has worn away over time.

A flutter of wings above my head announces the return of the crow. I stand tall and step back, squinting from the sun. It watches me with bead-black eyes and ruffled feathers, but I refuse to let it unnerve me. High in the tree, I spy what must be its nest: a messy rounded shape of straggly straw and twigs disguised within the tree's dark-green foliage. Poor thing's rearing chicks most likely. No wonder it's so protective. Until now it's had the run of the place. I doubt it's happy about people coming and going.

"I won't harm you," I say, "but you'll have to get used to visitors, because there'll be a lot of us over the next few weeks."

By means of an answer, it emits a loud *craaa* and shits. A white-hot splat lands just short of my feet. Damn crow!

"Tough old bird, aren't you?" I say, stepping back in case it does another, but I cannot help but laugh.

I turn around to face the church. Something beige hangs on the door handle, a bag of some kind. I hurry along the path, eager to see what it is. The cloth bag—the linen type they use in upmarket eateries—has been tied to the metal ring. Its neck is tightly bound with string, and a pale green label printed on the front of the bag reads: *Snip 'n Tucker Cafe, Bilbury.*

I place a hand beneath it, testing its weight. The contents feel hard and irregular, and the bag makes a clickety sound as I jiggle it. Glass?

Undoing the knot proves to be a nightmare, and I resort to using my teeth. At long last the knot loosens.

I peer inside. The bag contains twenty to thirty shards. But who put it here?

I gaze around at the cut grass, wondering if the gardener Hargreaves employed found the pieces while strimming and mowing. There is no accompanying note, so I have no one to thank; nevertheless, I'm grateful for the colorful gift. If this many pieces were revealed during the mowing, I might be able to find more.

Excitement rumbles in my stomach, and I remember skipping breakfast. In fact, I have eaten little these past few days, but now that I feel better, my appetite has returned. Decision made: I'll spend an hour here, then stop at the *Snip 'n Tucker Cafe* on the way home. That way I'll be able to ask which of their customers cuts the grass here, so that I can thank them. And if the library is open, I'll pop in there too and pick up the pamphlet. Kill two birds with one stone. The crow issues a harsh caw of disapproval, as if it heard my thoughts.

My search results in sixteen more pieces of glass, all of which need a thorough clean. As expected, the area close to the window is where most lay hidden, along with a few scattered elsewhere in the graveyard. I can think of no reasonable explanation as to how they got there and recall Hargreaves' words: *Here, there, everywhere.*

A few pieces are cracked or chipped, most likely from coming into contact with the gardener's strimmer. Fixable, so I'm not too worried. What concerns me more is that even with these extra pieces, I can still only account for about a third of the window. Unless some kind of miracle occurs, I'll need to replace much of it with new glass, but at least now I have a variety of colors to match to.

BY THE TIME I reach Bilbury, I'm famished. My stomach has given up rumbling and feels hollow. Scooped out.

As soon as I reach the High Street, I spot it: a cafe-come-sewing studio, judging by the contents of the window display. Jars of local honey and hand-woven baskets filled with edible goods nestle among bolts of fabric in shades of yellow and cream.

On a flagpole above the door hangs a sign bearing the cafe's name and a painted honeybee that looks so lifelike I imagine it flying away on the warm breeze.

A bell announces my arrival, and a middle-aged waitress greets me with a smile from behind the counter at the far end of the cafe. The aroma of coffee and cake fills the air, so I determine a flightpath around the tables, most of which are vacant, and head for the glass display, eager to see what treats are on offer.

"Good morning," the waitress says before glancing at the clock. "Or should I say, good afternoon?"

Behind the counter are two doors, both ajar. One leads to a tiny kitchen, the other to what appears to be a much larger room from which the soft whir of sewing machines and the hum of voices floats. The sewing studio, presumably. How nice it must be to live in such a community, I think, before the more suspicious side of me whispers to remind me how easily my mother would have slotted into such an environment. Surface appearances aren't always as perfect as they seem.

"What can I get you?"

The glass display cabinet is filled with both savory and sweet treats, including a handsome slab of sage, some honey and roasted-red-pepper cornbread, and sticky honey cakes drizzled in lemon frosting. The space between the plates is dotted with miniature pots of honey-butter and sprigs of dried lavender.

She sees me hesitate. "We have carrot cake, too," she says, pointing to a glass-domed plate on the countertop.

"Freshly made this morning." Her eyes twinkle, and mine are drawn to the cake.

It catches me off-guard, because it looks identical to the carrot cake my mother used to make: thick creamy frosting decorated with tiny carrots sculpted from orange fondant. The sense of nostalgia overwhelms me, and for a moment I'm filled with longing for home.

I should be sensible and order something like scrambled eggs on toast, but the cake has made the decision for me. The waitress senses it, too, because she removes the top of the glass dome before I can answer.

"Carrot cake it is then," I say. "And a pot of tea, please."

"Make yourself comfortable, and I'll bring it over."

I spy a little table for two in the front corner, near to the window, and make a beeline for it. I can more or less hide there. I always feel a little uncomfortable sitting in an eatery on my own. *Billy-no-mates*, I think to myself, but it's my own fault for being such a loner.

I drink in the room's décor as I wait for my food to arrive. On a small circular table draped in a dandelion print cloth are jars of royal jelly, beeswax and banana lip balms neatly displayed alongside little pots of propolis cream. It's evident that the honeybee is an important theme here, and it delivers a certain charm: quaint and quirky.

A middle-aged couple two tables away pay the bill and leave, and for a minute or so I am the only customer.

As the waitress approaches with my food, the doorbell tinkles, and in steps an elderly woman with a white cane.

"Afternoon, Lydia," the waitress calls to her.

"Beautiful day," the old woman says as she navigates through the higgledy-piggledy room with her cane before plonking down on the table opposite mine with a contented sigh. Her regular spot, I imagine, judging by the decisiveness in her step.

She leans the cane on the wall behind her and waits while the waitress finishes serving my tea and cake.

I glance across, noting the complete lack of pigment in the old woman's eyes. Bone-white sclera, devoid of both iris and pupil, nestle inside wrinkled lids.

"The usual, Lydia?" the waitress says.

"Yes please, Ava."

The old woman grins, not a tooth in her head. My guess is *the usual* must be something soft.

I pour my tea, dig my fork in the carrot cake, and take a bite. It's delicious, moist, and rich with just the right balance of fruit to cake.

"Tastes just like your mother made it, doesn't it?" the blind woman says, fixing me with her white eyes.

I swallow hard. How can she possibly know?

She chuckles. "Can't beat a good carrot cake, and Ava's is the best."

I put down the fork and chew slowly, my appetite waning. How does she know I'm eating carrot cake if she can't see?

She seems to sense my hesitancy, because she taps the side of her nose and says, "I use this. Never lets me down."

"Oh…I see."

She places a hand on her heart. "And this," she says, patting her chest. "The heart's pretty reliable, too."

I'm grateful for the reappearance of the waitress, who places a mug of hot chocolate on the table in front of the old woman.

"Not teasing my customers, are you, Lydia," she says, winking at me. The old woman chuckles and sips her hot chocolate, leaving a creamy mustache above her lip.

The waitress returns to the counter and busies herself with adjusting items in the display.

The old woman's white eyes bore into me, as if she is watching every mouthful I take, and all the while she grins. I squirm in the seat and convince myself I am being over-sensitive. Surely the remark she made about my mother was just her way of being friendly; she couldn't know anything about me or my background. And yet I still feel uncomfortable and can't wait to leave.

When my teacup is drained, I don't bother refilling it, even though the teapot is half-full. I finish the last bite of cake and return to the counter to pay. The waitress is brewing a fresh pot of coffee, so I stand and wait. Next to the clock is a cross-stitch tapestry in the shape of a beehive. Embroidered in bright gold thread are the words: The worker bees protect the hive.

"Everything all right?" she asks.

"Delicious, thank you."

I pay the bill and place the change in the little china pot marked "*Tips.*"

As I'm passing by the old woman's table on my way to the door, she grabs my wrist and holds it tight, her fingers cold as marble. "What the eyes don't see, the heart doesn't grieve," she whispers. Then, in a more gravelly tone: "Load of nonsense!"

I get the feeling she's about to say more, but something about her makes my skin crawl—the overly familiar gesture is unsettling—so I yank my hand from her grasp and leave quickly. The tinkling bell above the door cuts off suddenly as the door closes behind me.

Unsettled by the encounter, I head towards the car park, thinking only of home. But then I remember the pamphlet at the library. I turn on my heels and groan, my hackles already raised.

When I enter, the librarian is dealing with another customer, checking out the woman's books and engaging in affable conversation, but as I approach the counter, she catches sight of me and stops mid-sentence before recovering and carrying on. I wait until she has finished with the customer, then step forward.

"Yes?" she says, fixing me with her gaze. Today she wears a crisp white blouse and a starched demeanor.

"I've come for the pamphlet," I say. "The one about local churches."

She shakes her head and shrugs. "Local churches?"

"You put it to one side a few days ago. I said I'd come back for it but haven't had a chance until now."

A pause, then, "Do you recall the exact title?"

My face burns hot. "I don't, actually. It's the one with information about St. Sannan's." I lean across and point beneath the counter. "You put it on the shelf there and said you'd keep it for me."

She crouches down and rummages about, but her hands return as vacant as her expression. "I'm sorry, I don't recall. Perhaps I put it back on the shelf by mistake." She waves a hand towards the library shelves. "Go and look if you like."

I return to the local history shelf, knowing full well that I won't find the pamphlet there. I'm seething. First the woman at the cafe and now this. What is it with this bloody town?

My search offers no reward, just as I suspected.

"Any luck?" the librarian says as I'm passing by on my way out.

"No. It isn't there."

"Oh, I am sorry. I guess someone else borrowed it. But of course, without knowing the correct title there's no way of checking." The smile that plays around her lips refuses to match her apology, and I leave with my head bowed low.

SIX

SUNDAY MORNING DAWNS oppressive and humid, the air laden and heavy. The kind of weather that makes me listless. The heat has reignited my splitting headache, though thankfully not the nausea. I'm tempted to revisit the church and search for more glass, but I know how obsessive I can get if I don't keep it in check, and it is the weekend after all. I'd already dedicated my Saturday to the church and spent last night cleaning and catalogue the new pieces of glass I found, so I must refrain from returning today. One more week until I start the job proper. Until then, I need to find something else to occupy my mind.

I've always hated Sundays. As a kid, Sundays were riddled with rituals: attending church, Sunday lunch, and even, God forbid, *Songs of Praise* on BBC. My sister and I were forced to sit through all three tortuous events and were rarely excused without sound reason. All part of putting on a front as far as my parents were concerned. A *holier than thou* impression of a perfect life when the reality was far from it. Then, during the evening, the back-to-school rituals would kick in. Hair washed, shoes polished, bags packed. No wonder I associate Sundays with depression and find it hard to break through the gloom, especially when the weather's bad.

I try to lift my mood with a pain au raisin from the bakery and a couple of painkillers, then drive to Colebrooke and wander around the park, feeding the ducks and eating ice-cream. But seeing couples and families out together only increases my sense of isolation.

Almost a year has passed since I cut ties with my family, and I would not go back to the way things were, not for anything in the world, but it still hurts. Such a mixture of feelings: guilt, shame, sadness, but a sense of having been treated unfairly too; and not just because of what they did to cause the rift, but because of how they treated me my whole life.

Their behavior had torn Wren and I apart since childhood, and when they altered their will and signed everything over to her, they hammered the final nail in the coffin. For me, it wasn't the money that hurt; it was the betrayal. Wren didn't even have the decency to contact me to discuss what they'd done. She simply took the money and disappeared from my life without so much as a backwards glance. I wonder, sometimes, whether she feels any guilt at all, or has she convinced herself she did no wrong, that she was merely acting out their wishes?

My mother had phoned me out of the blue one Sunday morning, not long after I graduated, to tell me about their decision. I'll never forget the tone of her voice. I'd never contested a thing they'd given Wren, none of her cars or the deposit on her flat, and it was obvious my mother didn't expect me to contest this either. She'd always done my father's dirty work, fired his bullets, so to speak, so I wasn't surprised it was she who made the call.

Yet again they expected me to roll over and take their punishment, but this time I fought back. "I'm not surprised, Mum," I'd said without raising my voice. "I've always known it would come to this. Do whatever you want with your money, but don't expect me to give you my blessing. Those days are over." It was the one and only time I'd been brave enough to stand up for myself, and my parting words had shocked her: "By signing everything over to Wren, you cut me adrift, so I won't be contacting you again." I put down the phone before she could come back at me, and although I was shaking, it felt good.

They had lost their scapegoat, and I was certain they would try to make amends, because every narcissist needs a scapegoat in their lives. It's what feeds them.

Three weeks later, a card arrived in the post for my twenty-third birthday. A plain card, minus the word "*Daughter.*" Inside, my mother had written: "*Best wishes, Mum and Dad.*"

Their idea of waving a white flag. I guess they thought I'd make contact, but if anything, the insult cauterized the wounds and made me even more determined not to call. A month later, on Dad's birthday, I sent nothing, nor did I ring, and we have not been in touch since.

Over time, my therapist convinced me I was not to blame, that I'd done nothing to cause their resentment and that their behavior fit the mold of *The Narcissistic Family* to a T. All my life I'd done everything within my power to earn their love and approval, and in doing so I'd failed to recognize my own needs and desires. Pawns on a chessboard, that's all my sister and I were; but deep inside me lay a core of independence, one that eventually fought its way to the surface.

Still, as much as I enjoy my own company, there are times when life gets lonely and I miss having someone to talk to, someone to confide in and bear my soul. *Sometimes you'll need to do the reaching out, Robin*, the therapist had told me, so I sit on a bench and dial my friend Jules's number.

Her squeal of excitement is enough to lift my spirits. We haven't met up since I moved to Millbrook. Ridiculous, given that she lives only twenty miles away. I've known Jules my whole life, and, despite us drifting apart when I went to uni', we never lost touch.

"Come around," she says, once she calms down. "I'd love to see you."

"Sure you're not busy?" I ask, not wanting to make a nuisance of myself.

"Listen, you'll be doing me a favor. The boredom is driving me mad."

JULES SHRIEKS WHEN she sees me and hugs me close, while I stiffen in her embrace. I've never been demonstrative, but she's my best friend, so she understands.

"Good to see you!" she says, holding me at arm's length and drinking in every detail. "You eating?" She frowns and eyes me suspiciously "You look thinner."

"If you'd seen the pan au raisin I scoffed earlier, you wouldn't be asking that." I'm on the defensive, but her concern is endearing nonetheless. "Tell you the truth, it's been a rough week." I show her the scar on my index finger, which has already faded to silver in an attempt to hide its guilt. "Damn infection. Got into my system, I think. Made me feel lousy for a couple of days."

Despite my aversion to body contact, I hook my arm through hers and say, "Come on. Where are you taking me for lunch?"

When Jules asks what I've been working on, I keep it simple. "Doors and windows, the odd bit of studio work. You know how it is," I say and change the subject.

Truth is, the window is a puzzle I wish to keep to myself for the time being. I am entangled in the intricacies of its web, content with spinning one thread at a time until the web is complete. I've had little I can call my own so far in life, but this opportunity belongs to me alone. To share it might relinquish some of the magic.

Come now, Robin, my father's voice says, his tone haughty and mocking. *It's just a window. Get the job done and move on. Less head in the clouds, more feet on the ground is what you need.*

And just like that, a wonderful afternoon is marred by his presence.

When I'm halfway home, I realize I said nothing to Jules about the job at the church. *Why is that, Robin? Why do you always play your cards close to your chest?*

THE WEEK FLIES by in a busy blur, and on Monday morning I pull up in front of the church at eight o'clock at the same time as the builders. Heat rises to my cheeks as we vie for parking space. I am determined not to allow myself to feel vulnerable among these men, but having to reverse the van three times before I'm able to angle my van into a parking space is not the best start to the day. Eventually, one of them—a tall guy with a shaved head and an eyebrow piercing—comes to my aid by guiding me into the space and banging on the roof when I get too close to the stone wall.

I clamber out of the van feeling flustered. "Hi, I'm Robin," I say. "Here to restore the windows."

The other two, one squat and muscular, the other thin as a pin, say nothing, though I sense their eyes on me.

"I'm Christian," the one who helped me says. He points at the other two. "Matt and Arnold, or Arnie as we call him."

Arnold, the muscle-bound guy, flexes his bicep, which makes me squirm. I'm getting used to being a woman in a man's world, but such gestures bug me sometimes. I doubt he'd have done it had I been a man.

I peer over Christian's shoulder, wishing to divert our attention. Since my last visit, scaffolding has been erected and the roof is covered in a bright-blue membrane. Brand-new battens have been fitted, ready for the clay tiles that are already stacked in neat rows. I'm pleased to see they're reclaiming as many materials as possible.

He follows my gaze. "We made a start on the roof last week. Hoping to get it finished by the end of next week, weather permitting."

He returns to his van, which is three times the size of mine, and removes his toolbox, as do the other two. We're all of a similar age, judging by appearances: mid to late twenties. I grab four wooden trestles from the back of my van, hoist them up under my arms, and follow the boys through the gate and along the path.

The church is locked, and Christian struggles to open it.

"Don't suppose you found any pieces of colored glass while you were here, did you?" I ask, putting down the trestles.

"Damn key," he says, jiggling it about in the lock. "We had trouble with this last week too."

I whip the keys out of my pocket. "Here…mine works. I think Hargreaves gave me a master set."

"A few pieces," he says. "We left them on the altar."

I stand back to allow them to enter first before grabbing the trestles and following. "Hargreaves said you'd lend a hand to remove the windows. I hope he told you the same."

Christian tuts. "Don't be daft. No one tells us anything. We just turn up and get on with the job." He sees the look of discomfort on my face and grins. "It's no problem though."

I feel a little awkward. They must want to get on with repairing the roof, and I don't want to hinder their progress. "I'm sorry about that. I hoped he would have told you."

"Told the boss, most likely. You know what they're like." His smile is genuine and alleviates my guilt. "Right then, let's get the radio on and a brew going before we start."

We gather around the portable heater I brought and get to know each other over a cuppa, making idle small talk that gives little away, and then the three of them help me remove the first of the diamond-leaded windows and set it on the trestles in the chancel. Moments later they disappear, taking the radio with them.

Although I'm itching to start work on the stained-glass window, I know the sensible option is to repair these windows first. They will be far less labor-intensive, plus it will give me time to find the missing sections of glass.

True to their word, the boys have left six shards of glass on the stone altar: three bronze and three dark red. I tuck them into a pocket of my tool bag and ensure the popper is fastened before clearing the altar of debris and covering it in a sheet of thick polythene. I mutter an apology to whichever gods might be listening. The altar is sacred, and although I left religion behind at the same time I left my parents, I still respect the beliefs of others and the age and beauty of the building. However, in the absence of any other flat surface, I have no choice.

From the roof, the sound of Radio One and the roofers' banter combines with the rhythmic hammering of nails as they work. Preferring my own choice of music, I put in my earphones and select something more ambient. Soon,

I am lost in my own little world, free to daydream about how this place might look once finished.

The window I'm working on has six cracked panes that need replacing, but the leading is in good condition, as is the frame, which must have been replaced in recent years. All it requires is for the joints to be re-soldered. If the other windows are in a similar condition, each should take about a day to repair. Working on one at a time means each can be replaced at the end of the day rather than having to board the windows for the sake of security.

A tap on the shoulder makes me jump, and I turn around to see Jonathan Hargreaves standing there. I'd been so focused on the task that I'd failed to notice his arrival.

"Sorry," I say, removing my earphones. "I didn't hear you." He looks exactly as he did the first time we met. Same linen suit, khaki-colored hat, and purple-mirrored glasses, despite the day being rather gray. The bramble has been cut, so why is he still wearing the hat?

"Sorry I startled you," he says. "I just wanted to check you were okay and there's nothing you need."

"I'm fine, thanks," I say, looking straight at him. The glasses are off-putting. Because the glass is mirrored, his eyes are barely visible. "If this first window is anything to go by, I should have these repaired by the end of the week, then I can start on the stained-glass window."

"Good, good," he says, turning to face it. He folds one arm across his middle and rests his chin in the crook of his thumb and forefinger. "Find any more pieces?"

"Yes, someone—I assume whoever cut the grass—left a bag containing twenty-six pieces, plus I found a few more myself." I realize I forgot to ask the waitress in the cafe if she knew who the gardener is. Too hungry, I suppose, and then too flustered by my encounter with the blind woman. "Perhaps you could do me a favor and thank them on my behalf."

"Gron Jenkins, that'll be. He's the gardener-come-caretaker here. He's on the committee. I'll let him know." He pauses. "Any idea of costs yet?"

"Not yet. It depends on how much we need to replace, and what type of glass you want to use for the missing pieces. You have several options in fact, ranging from modern machine-made glass to hand-blown antique glass, or even something in between. Proper antique glass is made by traditional methods—hand-crafted and mouth blown—which makes it expensive. The colors and textures are exquisite though. You get to see the tiny air bubbles and striations, whereas modern glass is thinner and only textured on one side. As you can imagine, there's a big difference in price."

He rubs his chin as I speak. "Yes, yes. I understand, but the thing is, restoring the window is top priority, so there'll be no skimping."

I can't help but feel a little guilty, knowing that such projects are not easily financed, even with grants. "Well if that's the case, antique glass it must be. I could give you a rough estimate today if you like, but by this time next week I should have a much clearer idea of what will be needed."

He shakes his head. "No, no, next week will be fine. Anyway, I'll leave you in peace and go see how the roofers are getting on."

I watch him saunter down the aisle, still uncertain whether or not his motives are sincere. I'm sure it's just my unwillingness to trust, but there's something about him I can't quite put a finger on.

SEVEN

THE PAIN IN my head pulses to the rhythm of my heart, and all I want to do is sleep. I swallow a few painkillers, retching when they stick in my throat. I'm not usually sickly, but I've been plagued by headaches and a sore throat this last week or so. Perhaps the dust and mold in the church is the culprit.

I think back to when I was poorly as a child. Wren and I were given a spoonful of medicine and pretty much left to deal with it. But if my father was ill, it was a different story. My mother would mollycoddle him until he was well again. Did she simply have no nurturing instinct, or would he have been jealous if she'd lavished us with the same amount of attention?

The idea of breakfast makes me nauseous, so I sip a glass of milk instead. Headache or not, I cannot afford to stay home. I am determined to finish the last of the leaded windows today, so I fill a bottle of water and grab a pack of painkillers before setting off, a little late but nonetheless enthusiastic about the day ahead.

Parking is made even more difficult this morning as not one but two builders' vans are already there. I squeeze onto the grassy verge, tight against the stone wall, and am a bath of sweat by the time I exit the van.

The nave is a hive of activity. Matt and Arnie roar with laughter over some private joke that I'm glad I'm not privy to, while two new guys, and a woman dressed in overalls, a hard hat, and steel-capped boots do battle with the enormous rolls of damp-proof membrane that are balanced precariously on each of their shoulders.

I've grown fond of the boys over the week, but they've been busy working on the roof, so apart from a quick morning cuppa and a lunchtime sandwich, I've had little to do with them. The prospect of having to share the space with three more does not appeal, though it's good to have another woman here. We're still all too rare in the field of manual labor, in my opinion. She catches my eye as she passes and gives a wink of sisterhood, then all three of them disappear into the narthex through which I've just come.

The new builders are working at basement level. Rather them than me, I think, shuddering at the thought of the dank, dark space that lurks beneath the church. I set to work, glad of the earphones to drown out the banging that rises from below. An hour or so later, Christian yells from the door: "Robin, come and see what they've found in the crypt."

I hesitate, but since he has already disappeared back to the narthex, I feel obliged to follow.

In the far corner of the narthex, a trapdoor has been opened up in the floor, through which voices rise. Christian stands above the opening, grinning. The trapdoor, a roughly hewn piece of wood with a metal-ringed handle, gapes open.

Cold air seeps up through the gap, making me shiver, but it's not just the cold; it's the thought that he might expect me to go down there. I stand as close to the crypt's entrance as I dare, arms folded tight around my middle, and peer down into the darkness. A series of steep stone steps lead from the hole in the floor into the underground realm. I'm terrified of underground spaces and have never been inside a cave or traveled on the London Underground, nor do I intend to. Anticipatory anxiety, my therapist labeled it. She attributed it to the punishment my father used for my many alleged misdemeanors: locking me in the disused coalhouse in the basement of our childhood home.

The stench of stale air and sodden earth rises, adding to the dank atmosphere. Their voices echo below.

"They're making a start on the waterproofing," he says. "Come and see what they've found." He takes a step down but pauses when he sees I'm not following.

I step back. The hairs on my arms stand rigid, and my mouth is dry. "I'm not going down there. I—I don't like being underground." I'm annoyed with myself for being afraid. The last thing I want is to come across as a wimp, but the fear is real. Tangible. A cloying thickness that hangs in the air.

He beckons me forward. "It's okay. Nothing to be afraid of down here. No coffins or skeletons, I promise. They must have been removed a long time ago."

I shake my head and take another step back. "I mean it, Christian. I can't go down there."

This time he interprets my fear correctly, so he climbs back up and raises his arms in defeat. "Okay, okay… you don't have to. Thought you might like to see the room they found, that's all."

From the church bowels comes the sound of laughter and a scream. They're messing about, no doubt, trying to scare each other witless. Now and then a flash of light bounces off the wall, as if someone is holding a torch or lantern and moving it quickly.

The noise, combined with the thought of the crypt and that scent of stale dusty air, makes me quake.

"Shit," Christian says, studying my face. "The color's drained from you. All right, I'll tell you what they found. Save you going down." He takes a deep breath, as though trying to prepare both of us. "There's a bricked-up wall at the furthest end. Some of the bricks had worked loose, and when Jess gave them a knock with the hammer, they crumbled away. Beyond that is a chamber littered with bits of junk. Old books and candles, that kind of thing."

He watches me, judging my reaction. I sniff, wishing with all my heart that I was brave enough to explore this newly discovered realm.

"And there are drawings all over the wall. Words and stuff. Creepy as fuck." He shrugs and studies my face in the hope that I might have a sudden change of heart.

I can't deny that his words have piqued my interest, but my stance is firm. "Sorry, Christian. It's just—" I shiver and point towards the hole in the floor. "Do me a favor and take a few photos, will you?" And with that, I make a quick exit.

HALF AN HOUR later, I'm soldering the last of the leaded windows when Hargreaves comes striding down the aisle towards me. Shit, I mutter under my breath. I really want to get this finished, and it's been hard to focus since the crypt incident. I've spent the last half hour arguing with myself. I replace the soldering iron in its stand and attempt a smile.

"Just popped in to see how things are going." He nods in the direction of the narthex. "They're installing a waterproof membrane in the crypt, I believe. How are they getting on?"

At the mention of the crypt, I focus on the solder and pretend to brush off a stray fragment. "Fine, by the sound of things." I grimace at the noise coming from below, the sound of hammering and their raucous laughter. "Put it this way, they've been banging about all morning."

"Have you been down there?"

"Where? The crypt?"

"Yes, the crypt."

I shake my head but don't look up. "No. I've been too busy, and, besides, I don't like underground spaces."

"Oh…I see. Well, that's rather unfortunate."

I ignore his strange comment and, wishing to divert the subject away from the crypt, I point at the pane I'm working on. "Last of the leaded windows. The crew will help me install this later, then I'll be ready to start work on the stained-glass window on Monday."

"Good, good," he says, stroking his chin. "I can't wait to see that beauty restored. Well, I'll leave you to it and go and check on the boys."

I long to tell him there's a woman in the crypt, and to see his reaction when he sees her donned in steel-capped boots. Instead, I smile and tell him I'll have an estimate of costs ready by Monday.

I avoid the narthex all morning, just in case one of the gang teases me about the crypt. If Christian's told them I'm afraid of going underground, then they might.

When we come together for lunch, Christian introduces us to one another properly. The woman named Jess offers a high five but doesn't look me in the eye, which I find a little strange.

The others wander across to the other side of the nave to eat while Christian and I wait for the kettle to boil. I mention Hargreaves' visit and ask what he had to say about the bricked-up chamber.

"Didn't mention it," he says, scratching his ear. "In fact, he shouted down to us from the entrance. Guess he didn't want to get that linen suit dirty. We told him everything was fine, and he left us to it."

He dips the teabag, until the tea resembles the color of a copper penny, then perches beside me on an old pew, sipping from his mug. We sit in silence for a few minutes, watching the others laugh and joke across the other side of the nave like kids in a playground.

"I doubt there's anything valuable down there," he says, "so I guess he's not too concerned. Far as I can see, it's just builder's rubble and some old books. Oh, and Bibles of course. Stacks of them. They stink of mildew." He pinches his nose to prove his point. "Whoever bricked it up must have cleared it out first. That's my guess."

I blow on the surface of my tea, watching the liquid ripple. "Weird, isn't it? Why it was bricked-up, I mean."

"Sure is." He pauses. "Those drawings though." He feigns a shiver.

My stomach flips. The thought of strange drawings and words on the walls down there intrigues me, but I refuse to tell him this in case he tries to get me to go down there again.

"Anyway, how are you getting on? Think you'll be ready to start work on the big guy Monday?"

"I should be. I'll have the last of the plain windows finished this afternoon. Then, if you don't mind giving me a hand, we could remove the stained-glass and board the window before we leave."

"Course not. I was thinking though… might be a bit dark if we board it up. You plan on working in the chancel, don't you?"

I frown. "True, but I hadn't considered the lack of light once it's removed."

"Tell you what: leave it till Monday morning. I'll try and come up with an alternative. We won't be here next week because we're waiting on insulated plasterboard. Builders' merchants are having trouble getting hold of it."

My heart sinks. I'm not sure I fancy being here alone.

He sees my expression and tries to reassure me. "Don't worry, we'll call by Monday morning to take the window out and help you set up." He grins and digs me with an elbow. "Gotta laugh. When Hargreaves left, Jess followed him out because she needed something from the van." He cups his hands and calls across the other side of the room, interrupting their conversation. "Hey, Jess! Tell Robin what Hargreaves said to you."

Jess leans a shoulder against the wall and rolls an imaginary crumb between thumb and forefinger. "Fucking cheek," she says. She raises one foot and flexes it, as if about to kick a ball. "He had the nerve to ask if my feet ache from wearing these boots all day." She shakes her head.

Christian facepalms and chuckles, and the others erupt with laughter.

"Go on, tell her what you said to him, Jess," Christian says, wiping tears from his eyes.

She grins. "I said, 'No more than your head must ache from being squeezed into that hat, mate. She jabs a finger at Matt's forehead and shudders. "He's a freak, if you ask me. Can't even see his eyes when he talks to you."

Relieved as I am to discover I'm not the only one who finds Hargreaves odd, I find her manner offensive—a touch cruel, even.

Christian takes a last gulp of tea, then wanders over to join the others. I hear them mocking Hargreaves, imitating his mannerisms and upper-class accent, and my stomach churns. This is how my father behaved, and always behind someone's back of course. Not to their face. No, never to their face. Narcissists are cowards at heart.

When they return to the crypt, they do so without so much as a goodbye to me. I guess they could tell by my face that I wasn't impressed by their boorish behavior. Always the outsider, Robin, I tell myself. But if this is what being on the inside means, then I'd rather be the odd one out.

EIGHT

ON MONDAY, I arrive at the church by seven-thirty, eager to prepare the workspace for the removal of the stained-glass window. The old crow eyes me with contempt from a high branch of the yew and issues a warning as I enter the gate. Trespass! it croaks.

I pause on the path to admire the new roof: original tiles, now free of moss and algae, in keeping with the restoration. With the diamond-leaded windows repaired and the frames given a few coats of varnish, the exterior of the building stands proud. Most of the scaffolding has been removed, too, apart from at the back end where it will be needed so we can remove and replace the stained-glass window.

I enter the narthex, where the hole in the floor gapes wide, a cavernous mouth that I refuse to feed. All weekend, I've imagined what might lurk there, trying to convince myself to take a look. It's impossible though, I know that. My fear of enclosed spaces, and especially underground spaces, has its claws buried deep in my psyche and refuses to relinquish its grip.

I hurry past and enter the nave, now swept clean of nests and bird shit. It wears its brand-new ceiling joists with pride, a designer hat fit for a king. I'm pleased to see the renovations taking shape, but part of me yearns for the old. The decaying joists and the way in which nature had begun to take over the interior added character to the place.

I whip out my phone and take a few snaps of the building's progress to add to my website. Being part of the project team should add some kudos to my portfolio.

Christian isn't due to arrive for half an hour, so there's ample time to get the place ready. I face the stained-glass window, watching the eastern sunlight penetrate through the missing panes. It projects an image on the floor of the chancel, an elongated shadow of the leadwork's design that creeps towards the base of the altar. The few remaining pieces of colored glass display a kaleidoscope of color on the stone floor. The window will look magnificent once restored, but for now, it refuses to tell me its secrets.

My weekend's research had led me full circle back to St. Sannan himself. An Irish abbot by all accounts, and a friend of St David, patron saint of Wales. The only image I found depicted him holding a scepter, but no such an ornament is apparent here.

I take a few more snaps, then begin to assemble the trestles, laying sturdy wooden boards on top for my tools and the shards of glass. I cover the middle trestle with a clean white sheet and lay out all the sections of glass found to date in color-coded rows.

The altar will act as a mortuary slab for the stained-glass window. Fitting somehow, that the saint will be dissected and resurrected on a consecrated stone slab.

When the boys have failed to appear by eight o'clock as promised, I boil the kettle and try to steady my nerves with some chamomile tea. Without their help, I won't be able to remove the window or make a start. *Calm down, Robin. Christian promised he'd show.*

But a nagging doubt remains. They're off on another job this week. What if they've forgotten? After the frustrating weekend I've had, I wouldn't be surprised if they didn't show.

I take the tea out into the graveyard and perch on the old stone wall, facing the lane, to await their arrival. The ache behind my eyes persists, and the outbreak of hives on the back of my hands itches like crazy. Antihistamine hasn't helped, nor painkillers. I roll up my sleeves to see if the rash has spread, but thankfully it hasn't. Though what an ugly sight. If it hadn't been for the hives, I might have ventured further afield, to the library at Cirencester, in the hope of finding more information, but my hands look terrible, and the headache was severe enough to stop me driving far.

I roll down my sleeves and rest the backs of my hands on the stone wall in an attempt to soothe the itch.

By 08:15, there's still no sign of the van. Every minute feels like an hour, so I jump down and wander among the gravestones.

The grass has grown a few inches since it was cut, and it soaks my feet with early-morning dew, cooling my angst.

Most of the headstones are simple curved or pointed arches, and all are made from old stone. No marble. Burials here must have stopped before marble became fashionable. A few larger headstones have kerbs or footstones attached. I stop in front of one of the more elaborate stones and search for a name. There is none, but when I run my fingers over the stone, I detect a faint indentation. The lichen is too thick to see what it says, but a rubbing might help. At least it will keep me busy while I wait for the boys.

I head indoors and return with a sheet of paper and a stick of charcoal. When I return, the crow is perched on the headstone, watching me with its beady eyes. My footsteps are swift, yet it refuses to move until I am just one step away, then it takes flight and lands on another headstone a little further away.

I feel the surface of the stone until I find the indentation, then hold the paper with splayed fingers to prevent it flying about in the wind. Rubbing complete, I hold the paper skyward. An image of three overlapping curves, elliptical, eye-shaped, and in the center of each is a small circle. A pupil?

I'm about to repeat the process with the stone next to it when I hear the rumble of a vehicle. *Please let it be Christian!*

I hurry to the gates and am delighted to see his van.

"Sorry we're late, Robin," he says. "Had to call at the builder's merchants for a few things. I bet you were sweating."

My stress dissipates into thin air. "You had me worried, I must admit. Never mind, you're here now." I'm so pleased, I could hug him. But I don't do hugs.

Matt and Arnie stumble from the van, stretching their arms skyward and yawning. Christian raises his eyebrows and shakes his head. He's the most hard-working of the three, and often has to take the lead when it comes to motivating them.

"Right then," he says, rubbing his hands together. "Let's get this window out sharpish. Come on, boys, Robin's waiting to start." He nips around to the back of the van to retrieve a large sheet of Perspex, then leads the way along the narrow path, calling over his shoulder. "Thought we'd use this to plug the gap instead of boarding the window. You'll gain more light with this."

We set to work. The window's substantial size and fragility requires delicate handling, but the old frame relinquishes its jewels without too much of a fight. By nine-thirty, the old panel lies inert on the altar, awaiting its rebirth.

The boys fix the Perspex sheet over the window opening before they leave and promise they'll be back to start on the wall insulation as soon as the materials arrive, which will likely be towards the end of the week.

Alone again, I breathe a sigh of relief, grateful that I'm finally able to begin.

"Right then, you beauty. Let's get started." My voice echoes through the void, hollow and vulnerable, so I switch on the radio.

With Capital FM for company, I soon forget how alone I am and set to work on chipping out the old putty around the edge of the frame before giving the whole thing a rubdown with a brass wire brush and vacuuming off the dust. Now and then, the thought of the crypt edges its way in, but I push it out and focus hard.

I remove the old tie-bars with pliers, freeing the panel from its bounds. Much of the lead has softened over the years, as I predicted, so it will need replacing. But before I do anything else, I need to make a rubbing: a vital part of the process, and without any form of picture to guide me, the only way of replicating the design.

I lay a sheet of white paper on top of the pane and fasten it down. Working bottom to top, I carefully rub over the whole surface with a charcoal stick. Once I reach the top, I take a step back and view the result.

A figure, for sure, but first impressions suggest a strange-looking saint, if indeed it is a saint. What I'm seeing is more akin to the figure revealed to me on the computer screen. Six other figures stand beside it, three on each side. They stand in profile, their features too small to make out.

The main figure is leaning forward slightly, arms stretched behind as if about to leap from the frame. The torso is disproportionate to the legs—larger than it should be and malformed with a short neck and bulbous bony growths on each shoulder. Jesus Christ, what am I looking at here? Is this some kind of supernatural entity, or a disfigured saint? Whichever it is, it gives me the creeps. The hairs on my arms stand erect; my brain buzzes like static.

I close my eyes and try to remember the image on my screen. The figure had worn a cloak—oxblood red and cobalt blue. However, the rubbing depicts not a cloak so much as a wrap, a toga that starts at the chest then drapes loose, except where it's tied at the waist. My throat tightens; a feeling of unease churns in my gut.

I turn my attention to the figure's head: bare and bald and tilted skywards. Prominent cheekbones jut below the orbital bones and are asymmetrical. Its skull suggests it's covered in bony protrusions, just like the shoulders.

Worst of all is the grotesque tongue, which snakes from the gaping hole of its mouth all the way down the torso, where it narrows and curves to a point at hip-level.

My palms sweat and my breathing is labored. Something isn't right here. For a moment I have the urge to abandon the project, but that would be ridiculous. How can I be afraid of a pane of glass? But despite the unease, deep down lurks a sense of wonder: I have to see this thing through, if only to satisfy my curiosity.

I remove the rubbing and lay it on a bare trestle table, ready to annotate, when suddenly the door opens. Jonathan Hargreaves steps into the nave, raises a hand, and strides down the aisle, looking rather pleased with himself. The guy must have one set of clothes; he looks identical every time I see him.

He stops in front of the panel and rests his chin in his hand. "You've made a start, I see."

I smile and stand back so he can view it more clearly. "Yes. Though it hasn't turned out as I expected, I have to say."

He frowns. "What do you mean?"

"Look…here." I point him in the direction of the rubbing and watch as he studies the image. His thoughts are hard to read behind the mirrored lenses.

"Well, well," he says eventually, clearing his throat and reddening a little. "I see what you mean."

"It looks like some kind of malign deity to me…certainly not a saint."

He scratches his chin then folds his arms, his gaze still fixed on the charcoal rubbing. "I'm not sure I agree. It's rather unusual, I'll grant you that, but I wonder if it was meant to demonstrate the church's tolerance towards those who bear the mark of difference?" He raises an eyebrow, assessing my response, but I am lost for words. "On the other hand, it could be a warning against evil. You know, in the same way they used grotesques in the past."

"I don't follow you." I'm surprised by his apparent complacency.

"Well, take medieval art, for example. I read an article about a stained-glass window that depicted monkeys holding flasks of yellow liquid towards the light. Urine, of course." He glances in my direction. "I believe its intention was to satirize the medical profession, which claimed to be able to diagnose and cure all kinds of ailments by sniffing and assessing the color of a patient's urine. In fact, I'm sure such an example can be found in the Thomas Becket Miracle Windows of Canterbury Cathedral."

I get the impression he knows more about the art of stained-glass than he previously admitted.

"So, you think this window depicts what, exactly?"

He gives a haughty laugh which reminds me of my father. "I have no idea, but I wouldn't worry about it. All

I'm saying is that medieval church windows were not always devotional or solemn. Sometimes they included grotesque images and gargoyles too."

I am determined not to be outdone. After all, this is my area of expertise. "I'm well aware of that, but this window isn't medieval, is it? As I said before, I believe it dates from around the turn of the nineteenth century, a time when most stained-glass design depicted religious iconography or the botanical rather than the grotesque." A sense of unease creeps up the back of my neck and makes me light-headed.

He frowns. "Does it bother you? I mean, it's just a panel of glass, isn't it?" His tone is belittling and annoys me.

"No, it doesn't bother me," I lie, not wanting him to sense the degree of my discomfort. "It's just a little creepy, that's all." I raise both hands and take a step back. "Anyway, I'm sure it will be magnificent once it's restored. Now then…I've worked out the estimates." I turn to retrieve the folder from my backpack.

"Actually, I have some good news on that front." His tone lightens, and he rubs his hands together. Is this the reason he had seemed so pleased with himself when he arrived?

He clears his throat. "So…an old friend of mine owns a reclamation yard. We got talking over the weekend, and, lo and behold, he'd recently taken delivery of several stained-glass windows from a church in Devon. I asked him to hold onto them until I could visit, then popped down yesterday. I think you'll be thrilled."

He slips a hand into his jacket pocket and pulls out a sizable rectangular sliver of glass, cobalt blue and obviously antique. He offers it to me, and I take it from him and hold it towards the light.

"There's plenty more where that came from, and almost all the pieces are of a similar shape. The patterned windows were abstract, nothing fancy in the way of form, so you'll have a nice selection to choose from."

He sees the look of shock on my face and frowns. "I hope I haven't wasted your time. With the estimates, I mean."

"No, no. That doesn't matter at all." I am so taken aback by this lucky find that I don't know what to say. "But the colors may not match."

I turn around and retrieve a sliver of cobalt-blue glass from the selection on the trestle, then hold it next to the piece he's given me. A perfect match. My mouth falls open. "How strange…you'd swear they came from the same window."

He claps his hands and beams. "I knew you'd be pleased, and there's plenty more, I assure you. My guess is they were made by the same glassblower. What do you think?"

I shake my head, perplexed. "It's unlikely, though anything's possible. I mean, talk about coincidence though. Devon is miles from here."

"Hmm." He pinches his lip. "Anyway, he'll have the rest ready by this afternoon. In fact, I'm on my way to pick them up. Thought I'd check with you first, in case you didn't think it suitable."

"Suitable…it's perfect." The shard lies in the palm of my hand, a precious gift, though I can't quite believe it.

"He's getting one of his lads to disassemble the windows this morning. You'll find a good selection of colors, I promise."

I'm surprised by his flippancy and hold the two shards towards the sunlight again, almost hoping to prove him wrong. Same striations, same tiny air bubbles: a perfect match. But surely this is a chance in a million. Icy fingers creep along my spine. Is this coincidence or some sort of ploy? But how can it be? If Hargreaves was up to something he'd have handed the glass over before now, wouldn't he? I mean, I was ready to place the order. I heave a sigh. "Well, if the colors match and the pieces are big enough to make the cuts, it should work out well. See how it goes, shall we?"

The look on his face reminds me of Wren's expression whenever she got her own way, which was often. A semi-smirk, concealed beneath an innocent smile. "I'm sure you'll find there's ample to choose from, and possibly some to spare. Got them for a good price too. We go back a long way, you see, the reclamation man and I. And besides, he owed me a favor." Behind the mirrored lenses, I sense him wink, a momentary flicker of his facial muscles that makes the left side of his face contort.

"Anyway," he says, "I can see you're busy, so I'll leave you to it. I'll catch you later, hopefully. He flutters a hand in the direction of the paper rubbing and screws up his nose. "Oh, and don't worry about the design. It is what it is. Authenticity is all that matters." He touches the brim of his hat.

I stand, mouth agape, and watch him saunter down the aisle, head up and spine ramrod straight, without turning around.

I turn the volume on the radio down to zero and listen for his car pulling away. Ridiculous as it may seem, I am certain there is more to this whole business than meets the eye. Him finding the perfect glass is more than coincidence.

Old books, Christian had said. *Old books, and drawings scribbled on the wall.* Surely there must be answers among the chaos. I clench my fists and gather my breath for what I know I must do. The answers I seek might well lie beneath my feet, in the crypt.

Right then, Robin. It's time you faced your fears.

I march down the aisle and into the narthex.

NINE

"HELLO?" I PEER into the hole in the floor, legs trembling and heart racing. It's no good, I can't do it. And why am I shouting hello? There's no one here but me. My heart is a caged bird; invisible hands clasp tight around my throat and squeeze.

Once my echoing voice recedes there is total silence, not even a drip of water or the patter of mice fleeing. If I can bring myself to do this, I will have faced another of my fears. One step down, I freeze. My head swims, and my mouth turns to dust.

I am torn in two: the timid half does its best to talk the braver half out of descending these steps, while the braver half reminds me of how far I've come. *It's just an underground chamber, Robin. Think what you might glean from those scribbled words and drawings.*

Another step down and my legs fail me, crumpling beneath the weight of my body, but instead of fleeing, I slump down on the top step and stare into the void. I think back to last Friday when I stood at the top with Christian, seeing the torch beam bouncing as they moved about. But surely they couldn't have been working by torchlight? Shit, Robin, they must have used a portable generator to light the chamber. Idiot!

The empty plug socket stares back at me from the narthex wall. They will have taken the generator with them, which means all I have is my phone light.

I yank it from my overall pocket, switch on the torch function, and direct the beam in the direction of the crypt. Should I return tomorrow with a more powerful light source?

No, you must be kidding, Robin. You know you'll talk yourself out of it by then. Strike while the iron's hot, chicken shit!

I get to my feet, wanting to take another step, but the rest of my body refuses to comply. I close my eyes, and the memory of the coalhouse looms large, so tangible I can smell the mineral tang. I cough, recalling the dust that seemed to sit in my lungs for hours, my black-stained tears and snotty nose.

It's all in the past, Robin. A past you've escaped.

I open my eyes and try again, but my trembling legs refuse to obey. I picture myself fainting and falling into the darkness. I could break a leg, then I'd have to wait for Hargreaves to find me—if he turns up, that is. *Don't be ridiculous!* I slump back down on the second step and take a few deep breaths.

I know what I'll do. I'll shuffle down on my bottom. That way I won't need to rely on my legs.

I grip the phone tight and descend, one step at a time. Before I know it my feet touch solid ground. A wave of relief washes over me, but my palms are sweating and my mouth is dry as cinder. *One more step towards sanity*, I tell myself, only half-joking.

I shine the torchlight around the space. Silvery dust motes dance in the air, and the smell of damp earth invades my nostrils and taints my tongue. At the far end of the crypt, some thirty feet or so away, the remains of the brick wall are strewn across the floor near a gaping dark hole. On both sides of the main chamber, rolls of damp-proof membrane wait to be laid. As far as I can see, no skeletons or coffins are hidden in this space. It's just an empty shell, devoid of any horror except the worst kind: that which one's own mind produces.

I tiptoe the length of the chamber, glancing over my shoulder every now and then to ensure no one has replaced the hatch and locked me in. When I come face to face with the hole in the wall, I stop, unable to take another step. Beyond is a dark space, about eight feet square, and littered with rubble where Jess broke through.

The hole in the brick wall is half my height and barely wide enough to squeeze through. Without entering, I stoop low and shine the torch around the inside of the chamber. The vaulted ceiling sparkles white with efflorescence, likely the only jewels down here. Crossing the threshold seems like an insurmountable challenge, especially when my slick palms almost drop the phone, but the thought of finding out anything about the church's history is the sweet I desire. *It's just a freaking hole, Robin.*

Fists squeezed tight and teeth clenched, I step over the broken bricks and into the once hidden chamber.

Unlike the main vault, which has been stripped of furniture, the wall on the left is lined with shelves wide enough to have once stored coffins. Thankfully, none remain, but the thought makes me shiver nonetheless. I sweep the beam of light around. There are no bones or religious relics. The *junk* Christian referred to consists of a few lengths of old guttering, a stack of musty bibles, and a tin bucket containing sand and candle stubs.

I sweep the torchlight along the back wall. Efflorescence has turned the stone white, but it has some faint markings etched into it.

I cross the space in three strides and shine the beam on its chalky face. The outlines are barely visible, and yet…I squint and focus the beam closer. It can't be! Either I am going mad or the etching on the wall resembles the outline of the stained-glass window. I look again, tracing the lines of the figure with my finger. A head titled skyward, and there at shoulder level, the same bony protrusions as in the rubbing. The etching is cruder though, more like a sketch, and it has faded in parts.

I don't know whether to laugh or cry. Christian hadn't mentioned there was a depiction of the figure in the window, but then again, he hadn't seen the rubbing, had he? And even if he had, would he have recognized this as being one and the same?

A closer examination suggests a trailing tongue, but this is less clear than the overall outline. I scratch my head and try to focus. I realize that since I have walked the entire length of the crypt, the back wall must be beneath the chancel, which means the stained-glass window is situated directly overhead—above this etching. Coincidence?

I explore the rest of the chamber, examining the walls with my phone light. My heart skips a beat when, on the far right, my light shines upon some words written in a cursive font. I am only just able to decipher them. I read the sentence aloud: "Beware of he who shines in the light, for he is the devil incarnate."

Jesus Christ, what have I stumbled upon here? A quote from the Bible? If so, it isn't one I've come across before.

I turn my attention to the next wall, the one with shelving, but find no more words. The top and bottom shelves are bare, but on the middle shelf is a pile of old books. I sift through them, searching for anything of interest, aware that my phone battery is running lower by the minute.

Along with other religious titles, I find the *Holy Communion Preparation*, and beneath it, *Expositions of Holy Scripture*. Nothing that will tell me about the church's history.

Apart from the books, the shelf is bare. In a moment of madness, I trace my name in the dust: "*Robin.*" I'm half-tempted to add "*woz ere*" but refrain from acting on such a childish impulse. Instead, I trace out the silhouette of a robin, dotting its eye with my thumb. "Bring me luck," I whisper, half-believing it might come true.

I move onto checking the last wall, the one on my right, terrified that my battery will run out and plunge me into darkness. There are words on this wall too: words, letters, sketches too, but they are too faint to make out in the fading light.

An idea strikes, but I don't think I have the courage to carry it out. What if I were to take some photos? To do so, I'd need the phone's camera flash, which means I'd have to switch off the torch function temporarily. I feel sick at the thought of plunging myself into darkness, no matter how temporarily, but it's my only option.

A cursory glance at my phone informs me that only twelve percent of battery life remains. Not a lot, given the circumstances. I can't afford to waste time dithering.

I switch off the torch, expecting a total blackout, but the backlight provides a little illumination. I take several photos of the etched wall and the other walls. *Beware of he who shines in the light, for he is the devil incarnate.* Seeing the words pop up on the display gives me the shivers.

Okay, Robin, time to get out of here.

I switch the phone back to torch mode and head for the larger chamber. As I'm about to step through the gap, I notice that the old tin bucket, brimming with sand and topped with candle stubs, has an odd tilt to it. The slab on which it stands is uneven.

Dare I risk a few more moments? I re-check the battery: ten percent.

I move the bucket aside and test the slab with my foot. A rocking motion suggests it has been removed and replaced unevenly.

But when I kneel and try to find fingerholds to lift one end, there is nowhere to grip. I scan the space, but there's nothing slender enough to help me lever the stone from the floor.

I slip back into the larger chamber and shine the light around to see if there's anything useful there.

On top of one of the rolls of membrane is a pair of sturdy scissors. Worth a try.

I return to the slab. It takes some doing, but I manage to pry it up just enough to get a grip on it and lift one end from the hole. I upend the slab and prop it against the shelving.

My instincts were correct. Set into the floor is a hollow space in which rests a cloth parcel, bound at the neck with string.

I pick it up. Whatever is beneath the cloth is flat and solid. Books, by the feel of it. I use the scissors to snip the string and reveal the contents.

Three books. The top one is leather-bound and a little moth-eaten. In gilt letters, the words *Parish Records* are barely visible. I open the cover and shine my phone light onto the title page. It reads: *Register of Bilbury: Baptisms, Marriages, and Burials, 1800 to1900.* No mention of the church's name on the front, which is disappointing, but when I turn the page, I see: *Records for St. Mary's, Bilbury and St. Sannan's, Coppersgate Woods, formerly known as—*

The next word is illegible, having been scribbled over and over with thick black marker.

This must have been done in recent years, because such markers didn't exist back then. What is it about this place that makes people determined to hide its true name?

The paper is yellowed with age, and all entries are handwritten in immaculate cursive script. As far as I can see, there's nothing untoward about this volume, apart from the blotted-out name. A cursory glance further on reveals columns and rows of recorded dates, as expected.

The second is a notebook. On the first page are the words: *Reverend Peter James*. At last! Now I have a name to search, though my work here will be over in a week's time. If only I had found this earlier.

The third book sets my heart racing: a sketchbook, by the look of it. A series of hand-bound pages, the paper thick and textured, old and made of pulp. I shine my phone light onto the first page. There, in the center of the page, is a symbol. Three elliptical curves, each with a dot at the center—just like the symbol on the headstone.

I'm about to flip to the next page when a sound from upstairs startles me. I hold my breath and turn to face the main chamber. It comes again: a gentle rustle. Blood drains from my limbs; my fingers tingle. Frozen to the spot, I'm certain my heart is beating so loud it will give me away.

Silence ensues, but the feeling of being watched returns with a vengeance. I clasp the books to my chest and hurry back towards the steps.

Half expecting to see Hargreaves at the top of the stairs, I'm surprised to find the narthex empty. The front door is open, as is the door to the nave. But Hargreaves closed the front door behind him when he left; I would have noticed, had he left it open. Who, then, has opened it?

A gust of wind whisks up a tiny scrap of paper from just inside the doorway and makes it dance towards me. It rustles along the flagstones. Was that the sound I heard from down below? I doubt it. The paper is too small, the rustling too faint, for me to have heard it from the far end of the crypt.

I stoop to pick it up, but it dances away, glistening silver to white and back again. A chewing-gum wrapper, the same kind I gave Hargreaves the first day we met. I trap it beneath my foot, pick it up, and hold it between thumb and forefinger.

My phone number is scribbled on the white side. Did he drop it earlier?

Craning my neck, I peer along the path, but apart from my van the space is empty. Nevertheless, I step outside and scan the graveyard, certain someone is here.

A loop around the graveyard assures me I am alone, and the fresh air and daylight revives me. Books clasped tight under my arm, I slip the wrapper inside the pocket of my overalls. It brings to mind my father, who hated chewing gum. He called it common and banned it from the house. Little did he know I kept a stick of gum concealed in my coat pocket whenever we went to church, though I was never brave enough to chew it. Just knowing it was there was enough. My secret rebellion.

And now I have another secret to add to the list, for my latest act of bravery has reaped its rewards in the form of parish records, a personal notebook, an artist's sketchbook, and some new photographs.

TEN

AS MUCH AS I'd like to take a pew and trawl through my loot, Hargreaves will be back later and will expect to see progress. My phone is dead, so I plug it in to charge. I'll have ample time to review the images this evening, and they'll be clearer on a computer screen in any case.

I turn my attention back to the window rubbing. I start by outlining all leadwork lines with a 4B pencil to ensure they are distinct and then shade in the few pieces to color-match those that remain in situ in the glass panel. A touch of cobalt, a few daubs of sage-green, but mostly oxblood and sepia. Twenty-two sections in total. They hardly fill in any of the window: the majority of the sheet remains stark white, though I'm hoping the shards I've gathered so far will make a difference. Finding where they fit will be like completing a giant jigsaw puzzle or mosaic.

Hopefully, the glass Hargreaves brings will fill in whatever is left blank after that. For now, I remain skeptical. The piece he showed me matched, but that doesn't mean the rest will.

I run a hand through my lank hair and study the image. I'll rely on matching glass shape to penciled outline for the pieces of glass in my possession, which shouldn't prove too difficult, but how on earth will I know which colors to place in the missing sections? I guess I'll have to rely on good old gut instinct. Besides, who's going to judge?

If no one knows what the original window looked like, what does it matter?

Oh, it matters, Robin, my father's voice whispers in my ear, condemning my flippancy. *It matters very much,*

I start work on removing the last few pieces of glass before snipping away the soft leading. This part of the process is nerve-wracking, because, once complete, the window as an entity will no longer exist and will have to be assembled from scratch.

I wrap the twenty-two sections of glass in bubble wrap, tape the bundle, and tuck it into my backpack so that I can clean the pieces at home. A persistent tapping demands my attention. It's the old crow from the yew tree, pecking at one of the leaded windows. *Tap, tap, tap. Tap, tap, tap.* But when I approach the window, it takes flight.

After a quick snack, I spend the early afternoon renovating the original window frame. The wood is rotten in parts, but a bit of paint stripper and a few coats of varnish should make it sound. Hargreaves had stressed that he wants the renovation to be carried out in as environmentally friendly way as possible, with materials reused or reclaimed, and the frame is good enough to do just that.

Halfway through scraping off the old paint, I hear a vehicle pull up. No gentle rumble of wheels, but a larger vehicle. Christian had said the materials would arrive later in the week, but such plans often change. I put down the scraper and go to the door, expecting to see a delivery van.

Instead, I see an elderly man carrying a grass strimmer. He removes his cap and waves it towards the grass. "Gron Jenkins," he says. "Grown a bit, hasn't it?"

"Just a tad," I say, watching him hobble up the path. He favors the right leg, just like my pappi did. I'm secretly glad he's turned up. After this morning's debacle, the novelty of being on my own has worn off. It'll be nice to have some company this afternoon, even if it means I have to work with the hum of a strimmer outside. "I'm Robin Griffiths. I'm repairing the windows."

He stops a few feet from me and frowns. "I know who you are," he says. "Word gets around."

What a strange comment. I'm about to thank him for leaving the glass sections in the cafe-bag when he says, "I'm on the committee, see. We know everything that goes on around here."

He lays the strimmer on the grass, then stands hands on hips and points towards the leaded windows. "Done a nice job there. Fair play."

It crosses my mind that he wouldn't have made such a comment to a man, but perhaps I'm being overly judgmental. "I made a start on the stained-glass window today," I say. "I'm stripping the frame at the moment."

He nods, then picks up the strimmer again and tugs at the pull-cord. It kicks into action at the first tug, and the sudden vibration startles me. My nerves are fraught. He starts work, and it's too loud for me to thank him for finding the glass now. I would have invited him to see the window too, but it seems the discussion is over, so I head back indoors.

After a while, my ears grow accustomed to the hum of the strimmer, and I'm able to focus on sanding the wooden frame. The monotony of the task, being purely physical and requiring little thought, helps to calm my mind.

The buzz of the strimmer grows more distant, then slowly draws closer again. Eventually it stops, and a few moments later he calls from the door.

"Found a couple more." He holds out his right hand, palm up.

I hurry down the aisle, eager to see what he has found.

In his hand lies a flesh-toned piece of glass caked in mud and another that's reddish-brown, like dried blood.

"Ooh, thank you." I take them from him and hold the reddish-brown segment towards the light streaming in through a side window. Tiny pin dots stipple the surface, and I know instantly where the piece belongs in the design. The dots represent the papillae: the tongue's taste buds.

I am unprepared for what happens next. As I examine the shard, saliva floods my mouth. I swallow, a salty taste, yet sweet, too…sensual. Heat rises to my face, and my breathing is rapid. I plonk the section on the windowsill, keen to get it out of my hand.

I turn my attention to the flesh-toned shard. The response has made me nauseous; my attention is all pretense. And all the while Gron watches me, pale-blue eyes clouded by cataracts yet glowing with animalistic pleasure.

"Like what you see?" he says, grinning. His teeth are nicotine stained. The smell of marijuana tickles my nose as he laughs and coughs.

Not at all what I would expect from a member of a church committee in what must be his seventh decade. His demeanor makes me squirm, and I'm eager for him to leave.

The flesh-toned shard grows warm in my palm. It slips against my sweat and digs into my thumb-pad. I grip it tightly, then run my thumb along the edge, judging whether or not it would serve as a weapon if he were to attack me.

Instantly his expression changes. His smile radiates innocence. The scent of skunk dissipates and is replaced by that of freshly cut grass. The lustful flame in his eyes is extinguished, until all I see is an old man who reminds me of my Pappi, my mother's father who died when I was ten.

The glass in my hand cools. I release my grip until it no longer digs into my flesh and place it on the windowsill beside the other segment before taking a deep breath.

"You all right?" With a look of genuine concern, Gron holds out a hand as if to steady me. "Shall I get you a glass of water?"

"I'm all right. It's the heat, that's all." Deep breaths, in through the nose, out through the mouth. Three times, just as the therapist taught me.

He continues to stare.

I manage a tight-lipped smile. "I'm fine, really." I place a hand on my heart.

"Well, I'll be off then…"

I nod, and he touches the brim of his hat, a gesture of respect, just like Pappi used to do. My throat constricts, and I have to fight back tears. What I wouldn't give to see Pappi again. Out of all my family, it's only him I truly miss.

"As long as you're sure you're all right?" he says.

I cannot answer him, because I'm afraid that if I speak the tears will spill, so I turn towards the window and pick up the shards of glass: two benign slivers of fused silicate—nothing more. Everything else must have stemmed from my imagination.

I watch him hobble down the path, dragging his left leg behind him. He hums a tune that carries through the open door. "Rock of Ages," Pappi's favorite hymn.

In between coats of varnish, I turn my attention back to the window, still a little shaken. Now that I have a paper template to work from, I can begin to place the shards in their correct positions. Several have cracked and will need to be repaired. Some of the broken-off fragments are missing, so these will need to be color-matched and fixed. However, it's a delicate operation, one that requires a steady hand. I decide to leave this task for another day and make a start on the border, which should be much easier.

The panel is bordered in sable-colored glass, textured with a ripple effect. I know this because several of the found pieces are simple rectangles, regular in size, that fit the rubbed design perfectly. Even so, it takes a while to locate their matching place on the stencil. The slightest difference in tone or size can make a world of difference to the overall effect, and when working with antique glass, one rarely finds uniform pieces.

The radio plays quietly in the background, the volume low enough that I hear the sound of a car. Hargreaves, I assume, returning with the glass. The books are propped against a pillar, so I slip them inside my backpack before he enters. A pang of guilt hits me, because in truth they belong to him, not me, but I must examine them before I hand them over. Since I'm the only person who knows of their existence, I'm unlikely to be discovered, and I can always pretend to have found them at a later date.

I straighten and face the entrance, hoping my guilt doesn't show.

I am surprised to see him empty-handed. I'd expected him to be laden with treasure.

He raises a hand and leans against the door, a little out of breath. "I wonder if you might lend a hand," he says. He rubs his wrist, a pained look on his face. "The arthritis is playing the devil with me today, and I'm afraid I might drop the box if I try to carry it on my own."

I hurry down the aisle to join him, hoping that putting a distance between me and the contents of my backpack will help quell the heat that has risen to my face.

The boot of his car contains three sizable cardboard boxes—not the sturdiest method of transporting cargo as precious as antique glass, so we'll need to take care. He uses his car key to slit the tape off the box on the left and unfolds the lid. A layer of polystyrene packaging chips conceals the shards beneath.

He rummages through, a game of lucky dip, disturbing several bits of polystyrene which pop out of the box into the boot.

"Careful they don't cut you," I say, eager to see what's inside.

"Gron's been here by the look of things," he says, nodding in the direction of the churchyard as he pulls out a large ocher shard. "Grass grows quick at this time of year."

I ignore his comment about the gardener and take the piece of glass from him. It covers the whole of my palm, which pleases me. If the majority of the pieces are this big, I'll have more chance of making accurate cuts. "Nice." I hold the shard skyward, taking care to avoid aiming it at the sun. I can tell it's old by the tiny air bubbles and variation in color. The shard ripples ocher to golden tortilla, making me hungry to see the rest.

"Pleased?"

No need to ask, he can tell by the smile on my face. "Are they all around this size?" I say, beaming.

"Yes. Some are a little smaller, but most are at least this big, and the colors are exquisite. I can't wait for you to see them."

Together, we carry the boxes up the path and all the way to the chancel before placing them carefully on the floor near my workstation. The effort exerts him. He rubs his wrist and grimaces, and I think to myself, why are you afraid of him, Robin? He's just an old man.

Gron's face swims in my vision, reminding me of how I allowed my imagination to get the better of me this morning. Shameful. My adventure in the crypt, the chewing-gum wrapper, the unusual gravestone rubbing: they all made me open to suggestion, that's all.

"Mind if I take a look?" I say.

"Not at all. They've been cleaned too, by the look of them."

I rummage inside the opened box and pick out two or three shards: one ruby-red and crystal clear, one a pale shade of lemon that reminds me of boiled sweets and makes my mouth water, and the third a coppery bronze shade. The quality of each is excellent, and I admit that I underestimated him when he told me about the find yesterday.

"Do you know, I feel like a kid at Christmas."

He smiles, then pinches his lip in the manner I am becoming familiar with. "I knew you'd be pleased. It's not just the savings we've made, but the glass comes from a recyclable source that pleases me, you know."

His sunglasses are misted, but instead of wiping them he looks down his nose, attempting to see through the small gap. I wonder if the glasses are a way of hiding some kind of deformity. Perhaps his eyes are scarred in some way. It's unusual for a man of his age to be vain enough to put up with being unable to see rather than show his face.

He gathers himself together and steps forward to study my work. "Coming along nicely, I see."

The border is half-finished, but the middle of the design remains bare, and I feel the need to justify why I've completed so little to date.

"It took a while to remove all the old leadwork and strip the frame. Look—" I point towards the frame, which stands on a dust sheet, propped against the back wall. "Another coat or two of varnish and it'll be ready."

"Very nice. Listen…" He glances at his wrist watch. "I have a meeting at five, so I'd best be off. I'll catch you later in the week, okay?"

"Of course." I'm secretly glad he's not sticking around, as I want to scout through the boxes of glass in peace. A memory springs to mind—a memory of birthdays and Christmases and how I always preferred to open what few gifts I received alone so my parents wouldn't see the look of disappointment on my face.

Halfway down the aisle, he stops and turns to face me. "Do you know if the boys have fixed the light in the crypt? I want to take a look around in case there's anything of interest down there."

I think about my earlier adventure, and panic. What if I've left some evidence behind?

Shit, I forgot to replace the slab. In my hurry to leave it slipped my mind. "I—I have no idea, sorry. Like I said, you won't catch me down there." I giggle nervously.

"Ah well, I'll check it out. I have a torch in the boot of my car." He wanders off, leaving me with a drum for a heart and three boxes of antique glass.

He returns from his car and goes down to the crypt. My hands tremble as I kneel in front of the boxes, listening to him shuffle about beneath my feet like a rat under floorboards. Instead of looking through the box, I anticipate his every move, wondering how long he'll stay. He's taking his time, though there's little to see. I've removed anything of interest. If he has a meeting to attend, surely he won't stay much longer. *Come on, come on…please leave!* I hold my breath and listen.

His footsteps fall silent, and I close my eyes, picturing the scene: the writing on the wall, the stack of Bibles, the upturned slab that reveals a hole.

And then I remember…the word I wrote in the dust: *Robin*. How stupid! The image of the robin I traced in the dust winks. The evidence is there for all to see. By writing my name in the dust, I've incriminated myself.

Liar! It is my father's voice that chastises me, not Hargreaves'.

A minute or so later, he ascends the steps to the narthex. Half expecting him to challenge me, I am relieved when he calls from the door to say he's leaving and offers a simple wave. No eye contact though. Does this mean he suspects something? The builders could be to blame for the upturned slab, but if he saw my name in the dust? That's another matter altogether.

The moment I hear his car pull away, I unplug my phone from the charger and hurry down the aisle. With any luck, he might not have noticed, but what if he makes a return visit to the crypt? My phone is fully charged, so at least I have light. As much as it pains me to return to that dark underground space, I must replace the slab and wipe away all evidence of my guilt.

ELEVEN

AT HOME THAT evening I settle on the sofa with the looted treasure stacked beside me. From what I could gather when I returned to the crypt, Hargreaves had left everything undisturbed. The upturned slab, my name in the dust. I'd replaced the slab and swiped away my name, hoping he hadn't noticed, though time would tell. Now, which to study first? Notebook, Parish Records, or sketchbook? The notebook, I think. I'm keen to discover more about the former reverend.

An internet search for *Reverend Peter James, Bilbury* provides scant information other than confirming he presided over both St Mary's and St. Sannan's from 1982 until his death in 1995. Nothing remarkable there. I know from my own experience that as churchgoers diminish in number, ministers often preside over more than one church.

More interesting is the fact that he was not replaced after his death, at least not at St. Sannan's. A new member of the clergy was appointed at St Mary's, but St. Sannan's was abandoned. Perhaps so few people attended such an out-of-the-way location it wasn't worth the upkeep.

I search for *St Mary's, Bilbury* and discover that a Rev. J Meredith now presides there. Might it be worth trying to talk to him?

I consider it for a moment, but what is the point when my work will soon be finished. If I'd discovered this lead earlier, I might have pursued it, but now there seems little point in doing so.

What kind of man was the Reverend Peter James? I turn to his notebook, expecting to read about church fetes and hospice visits. I am surprised to find the first page begins with the words: *Something sinister stirs within these walls. Something ancient.*

I curl my legs beneath me on the sofa and take another sip of tea.

The very first time I delivered a sermon at St. Sannan's, I knew something was amiss. The sun blazed in through the stained-glass window behind me—the window depicting the demonic deity—and penetrated my robes until perspiration soaked my back and my vestments stuck to my skin.

He's referring to the window I'm working on. A window with a demonic deity: it can be no other. Goose bumps spread up my arms, making me shiver. I hurry to the bedroom and grab an old fleece before returning to the sofa.

Thirty or so parishioners sat in the pews (a remarkable number, especially considering the church's remote location), watching me dab at my brow with a handkerchief. There was a look of discomfort on their faces, a look that told me they recognized my suffering and wanted the sermon to end as much as I did.

My first sermon.

What an impression I made. A sopping mess.

Had I been a young minister, one newly ordained, I would have put it down to nerves, but that was not the case. At the age of fifty-eight, I had already served for more than three decades, so it was not that.

It has taken thirteen years for me to finally admit that it was all because of the window.

He writes that the church was built on an ancient Pagan site of worship. Nothing unusual for this part of the world. Many Christian churches are built on such sites; in fact, the one seems to have evolved out of the other, but no other church, as far as I'm aware, can lay claim to the kind of things he describes next.

It was with a heavy heart that I returned the following Sunday, and had it not been for the help of Our Lord I would not have done so. But He had delivered me to this parish, and I couldn't fail Him. The Lord, it seemed, had decided this was to be my trial, the cross I must bear and the test of my faith.

Needless to say, it did not get easier.

Whispering voices rising from the crypt, malicious laughter and chanting in foreign tongues that filtered through the air vents. But there was no one there. Only the wind in the trees and the chatter of crows. And yet, wherever I went, the sense of someone watching me came too.

I grew fretful and beseeched God to help me in my hour of need. There were times when He would deliver, when blackbirds would sing and the sun would warm the golden stone. Times when parishioners would speak kind words and turn my fear to dust. Such times made me reconsider my state of mind, the sense of persecution, the isolation. And so it was that I accepted my duty and battled on until I could take no more.

Until I was certain.

My breathing is rapid, and the hives on the backs of my hands burn hot and creep along my forearms, causing the skin to erupt. Calm down, Robin, or you'll end up looking like a plague victim. Hives are nothing new to me, but I don't recall ever having such a vicious outbreak as this.

In the next passages, the reverend mentions items going missing, sudden changes in temperature, strange smells. One sentence stops me short.

I unlocked the door, stepped inside, and was immersed in the smell of the sea, though the church is many miles from any body of water.

His description takes me right back to the moment I held the shard of glass Gron had passed to me—that salty tang that flooded my mouth.

I read on. The reverend describes performing a christening where, having made the sign of the cross on the infant's forehead, he looked down to see a cross of blood, not holy water.

The look of horror on the parents' faces remains with me to this day. How could I explain such a thing? How could I tell them that the demon behind us had turned Holy water to blood?

It was *him though. His mirth surged through me like a knife through butter as the child kicked and wailed in my arms.*

I excused the incident to the parents by pretending I'd cut my thumb, but of course that was a lie.

On the next page, he had written about a wedding, where the bride and groom were about to exchange vows.

The first word, "I," was all the poor groom managed before his throat seized entirely. Time and time again, he opened his mouth to speak, but the words refused to pass his lips. At first I thought him nervous, but when his face burned red and the muscles in his neck bulged, I realized it was more than that. His bride squeezed his hand tight and, thinking him anxious, attempted to speak words of encouragement, but the beast behind us had stolen her power of speech too.

During all of this, both choir and congregation watched impassively, as though blind to the strangeness of the situation. They too had been enchanted.

Only when a flash of lightning and a clap of thunder broke the spell were they able to speak. I glanced towards the window and saw the deity lick its lips with its terrible tongue, and in that moment I knew…it was he who had interrupted the ceremony, he who charmed the congregation and made them ignorant of their surroundings, for not one of them so much as flinched, not even when the bride put her hands over her ears to drown out the thunder. Not even when her voice returned, and she let out an unholy scream.

Is it possible he was telling the truth? Was it just his imagination? Surely a glass image cannot become sentient and cause such havoc.

I recall my own response when I first saw what the window depicted, how I'd shuddered with distaste. But such a response does not mean there are supernatural forces at play. Once the window is restored and the sun shines through it, I'm sure the image will spring to life, but not in the breathing, thinking sense. It will only be as alive as any artwork when coupled with the power of imagination and the trickery of the sun.

If the clergy believe in God, then they are equally as capable of believing in the devil. In fact, most do. Over time, the image in the window got to him, that's all. I'm not sure I'd want to stand at the altar delivering the word of God knowing that such a deity stood behind me, watching… listening—if only in a glass image.

In some entries, Reverend James also seems to question his own sanity. He talks about how some of the things he witnessed followed a sleepless night, or after having left the bedside of one who passed on. He admits to being forgetful and careless on a few occasions, becoming a danger to himself and others because of his absent-mindedness, and I am more and more inclined to think the man was ill.

He speaks of his disappointment when certain parishioners, who he refuses to name for fear of reprisal, use the church to promote themselves within the admirable community, and he hints at one person in particular who he insists shall remain nameless.

I am too afraid to name him here, for I believe in my heart he is in league with the demon in the window, and that should his name appear in writing I will be severely punished.

I think back to my childhood, to my own parents' attitude to religion and the way in which they used it as a disguise for the mistreatment of their own daughter. Or daughters, I should say, because Wren was a victim, too, in some ways. Outwardly as frail and fragile as the little bird she was named for, they poisoned her against me, turning her into the money-grubbing, cold-hearted thing she has become. Wren was encouraged to tug and tug at the worm in the ground until she bit off its head.

To outsiders, my parents presented an image of the perfect family, holier than thou, and persuaded most people who knew them of the same. What would their friends have thought if they knew they punished me by shutting me in a dark hole? What would they have thought of the scripts my father kept locked in his library? Scripts he poured over night after night. Scripts I knew were not of the faith, or why else would he ban us from touching them? Night after night, he would insist we learn a passage from the Bible and recite it word for word before being allowed supper, so holy books were never off limits, only those he kept under lock and key. Oh, how easily people can be persuaded to fall for an image. How easily others are taken in by a manipulator such as my father.

Only Pappi suspected that my father wasn't all he pretended to be, but Pappi died before I was old enough for him to come to my rescue. I know he recognized it though. I saw it in his eyes, in the sympathetic looks he gave me as he ruffled my hair, and in the way his eyes lost their sparkle whenever he spoke to my father.

Now, as an adult, I understand that his hands were tied. Had he spoken against my father, my mother would have cut him out of our lives altogether. Perhaps Pappi knew it wasn't worth the risk. Maybe he hoped that one day, if I needed him, he'd be able to help.

It is true evil, when a family turns on one of its own, ostracizes the chick who begs for food. But what happens when, despite all odds, the chick survives and flies the nest for good? The final entry in Reverend Peter James's notebooks, which he wrote on February 21, 1995, causes my heart to skip a beat.

I know now that I cannot destroy the deity; it is not within my power. It has lived too long and has grown too powerful. It takes possession of our senses, causing us to hear what it wants us to hear, feel what it wants us to feel, smell what it wants us to smell. And those eyes! Blind yet all-seeing!

I'd heard a phrase like that before. What was it the blind woman in the cafe said to me as I was leaving? What the eyes don't see, the heart doesn't grieve. Those were her words. A common enough saying, but she'd followed it up by declaring it a load of nonsense. Did she mean that what one couldn't see might still be felt on an emotional level after all. And was she referring to herself? Or me?

I remember the touch of her cold hand on my skin, the grin on her face. I push the uncomfortable memory aside and return to his final pages:

It even has a doppelganger, down in the crypt. A much cruder version, etched into the stone. Time and time again, I have tried to erase it, but the chisel skids across the surface of the stone until all I achieve is bleeding knuckles.

The etching! I sit up a little straighter as I read on.

So no, I cannot destroy it. What I can do, however, is destroy its image, the one in the window, that which sunlight breathes life into, and hope that in doing so I am able to stall its advance.

Yes, most would think me mad and would have me sent to an asylum. But I am not mad, and I will serve the Lord and my flock in the way I see fit.

In place of a Bible and crucifix, I will employ the tools of Jesus the carpenter and resort to a hammer and chisel.

Does this suggest the reverend broke the stained-glass window? Hargreaves had said the church had stood derelict and unattended for twenty-five years. That number coincides with the reverend's death. Could it be that his death was the catalyst for closing the church? So many questions!

I put the notebook aside and turn my attention to the Parish Records. The last entries in the register date from 1900, almost a century before the reverend's death.

So why were the two books hidden together? Did Reverend James hide the books before his death, or did someone else want them hidden? And why hide them beneath the floor?

None of it makes sense.

If it was the Reverend James himself who hid the books, he wanted to keep this parish register secret as well: there must be something of interest within the pages.

I glance at my phone and groan: 00:35. I have to get up for work in six hours, so dare not start on this document. And then there's the sketchbook, plus the photos. If I tried to get through everything this evening, I'd be awake all night.

I place the book on the coffee table and sit quietly for a few moments, considering what I have learned so far. Rather than providing answers, these books have left me with more questions than I started with. Did the reverend hide the notebook so that his words would remain behind after his death?

I prepare for bed in a trance, and, once I turn in, I'm reluctant to switch off the lamp. One thing in particular bothers me: If the reverend broke the window, did someone punish him for his actions?

But who? Hargreaves? I picture the crumpled linen suit and khaki hat, like Hercule Poirot in *Death on the Nile*, and chuckle.

I'm not aware of any connection between Hargreaves and the church prior to purchase, and yet there could be. It is possible, likely even, that Hargreaves attended St. Sannan's and knew Reverend James, and yet he has never mentioned him

His obsession with the window is suspicious. I understand him wanting to see it restored to its former glory, but couldn't he have had me create something new? Something more in keeping with a place of worship, or even something more modern?

And the glass—what are the chances of him having an acquaintance come up with the exact same colors and textures just when I needed them?

The heat and stress turning my hives to what feels like bee stings. I throw off the quilt to try to cool down. Surely, I am putting two and two together and making five.

Those words, though…the words the reverend wrote towards the end of his notebook: *I am too afraid to name him, for I believe in my heart he is in league with the demon in the window.*

Who else was involved in whatever was going on in the church back then?

TWELVE

AN OPPRESSIVE HEAT hits the moment I step into the street, coating my skin in a slick residue. I'm not surprised. Having tossed and turned for hours in the humidity last night, I'd got out of bed and opened the window at three in the morning, but it had offered little respite.

Eventually I'd managed to fall asleep, but the dreams! In one, my father had stood at the pulpit, his mouth moving but emitting no sound. His hands made wild gestures in the air and his face was red with fervor. I sat in the front pew all alone, wondering why he failed to realize his voice produced no sound, but when I turned around, the congregation was listening intently to what he had to say. Each one, their gaze rapt and full of adoration, devoured every word he spoke.

A tug at my heel had drawn my attention down to see my sister, Wren, curled like a cat beneath the pew. She caught my eye and giggled, opened her mouth and spewed a clew of worms, some bitten in half, still writhing, others whole and speckled with earth as if she had dug them up fresh.

My father looked down on us, saw her there grinning and worm-ridden, and laughed. His laughter grew louder and louder until it filled the nave all the way to the rafters, and the congregation laughed with him, coughing-up clods of soil and choking on earth and tears and pointing at me.

Wren, whose flesh became feathers, whose arms became wings, took to the air and flew towards the window. The window depicting the deity. Her tiny body hit it with such force it knocked her to the ground. She lay there, her right wing twitching for a few seconds, until she took her last breath. My father picked her up and cradled her in the palm of his hand, whispering words I could not understand. Then his knuckles turned white as he squeezed, crushing her body before throwing the tiny corpse at me. The slap of wet feather against my chest jolted me awake, and my eyes sprang open, half expecting to see Wren standing in front of me.

The dream is as sharp as a knife. The final image so keen it threatens to slit my throat and watch me bleed. But I have done so already by shedding my family ties. I will not allow it to kill me twice. Why a preacher though? My father has never preached. I guess my brain interpreted what I read in the reverend's notebook in such a way as to make it personal.

As I drive, I turn up the radio and the air conditioning, relishing the rebellious volume and blast of air that makes my eyes stream.

When I switch off the engine and step out of the van, the sudden silence is so thick it curdles in the heat. Oh, how I wish the boys were here!

I grab my tools and backpack and enter the churchyard, eyeing my surroundings for signs of foul play. Of course, there are none. The sense of foreboding is down to my overactive imagination and the nightmare, nothing more than a subconscious interpretation of what I'd read in Reverend James's notebook the previous night.

I am unused to the church interior being warm. It usually has a stone-cold heart, but the heat over the last few days has been oppressive, and the walls of the church have allowed the sun to penetrate their shell at last. The crypt's maw gapes open and offers a breath of stale but cool air in contrast to that which dwells within the church.

Despite having my sleep disturbed, I feel calm and ready to take on the task. I'll have the radio on low in the background. That way I won't have to keep selecting tracks and will be able to hear if anyone arrives.

My hands are steady enough to repair the broken pieces this morning, so I'll start with this task. Some slivers are beyond repair and will require new pieces to be cut, but several are worth saving. A little patience and the right tools are all that's required.

While I wait for the sections to dry, I start matching the others to the shapes on the paper stencil. This will tell me exactly how many pieces need to be cut from the reclaimed glass Hargreaves provided, and I'll have a better idea of which colors to use.

This is the exciting part: the part of the process I've been longing to tackle ever since he first contacted me. The task is like completing a jigsaw puzzle, nothing more complex than that, and yet it demands my full attention. Slight differences in tone require many shards to be placed and re-positioned, because much of the background consists of geometric shapes of similar size, all of which are colored ocher, sand, or flaxen. And it's not just tone but texture I have to consider too: some slivers are more dimpled or have more air bubbles, while others are smoother and clearer.

For the rest of the morning, I am engrossed in a kaleidoscopic world of crystal, and forget my troubles for a while.

Just after midday, I take my lunch outside and perch on the old stone wall, facing the woods beyond the church boundary. The sun catches something on the stone close to where I sit. Something has been placed there.

I wander over and pick it up. It is a child's hair clip, silver and shaped like a butterfly. The church has had visitors, perhaps? I pocket the piece, then return to my spot.

The flute-like song of the blackbird charms me with its spell while the repetitive call of the wood pigeon offers a meditative pattern on which to focus. The heat has made both listless, it seems, as there is barely a flutter among the trees.

My bottled water is tepid and tastes brackish, so I replace the lid and jump down from the wall. A few brimstones and the odd red admiral arrive in search of nectar among the wildflowers and weeds, and a bumblebee, its baskets swollen with pollen, buzzes by on its way home. Other than that, I am alone with the dead and my thoughts.

I amble about the headstones, following in the wake of the butterflies, searching again for any sign of inscriptions. The moss is a masterful magician and erases any trace beneath its sandwich of fungi and algae, but beneath the yew I find a fallen twig with a pointy tip. A useful tool for removing moss.

I set to work on the nearest headstone, though each clump of moss I remove feels like an act of vandalism. I mumble an apology to both the moss and whoever lies buried beneath.

All that my efforts reveal is yet another symbol: the same one as in the rubbing I'd made: three overlapping circles, each with a dot at the center. No name, no epitaph to remember the dead.

The headstone next to it reveals the same. By now I am certain they all bear the mark. I wonder if the sketchbook, which bears the same symbol on its front cover, will reveal more when I read it this evening.

By late afternoon, my stash of glass has dwindled. Only the slivers I repaired this morning remain. The warmth of the day has helped the glue to dry, and I am able to position them in the mosaic.

I stand back to admire the fruits of my labor. A little less than half of the design is filled, mainly the border, the background, and parts of the deity's robe, but not yet the more detailed areas such as its face or the smaller figures that stand beside it. A little disappointing, I must say. Completing the task will stretch my capabilities to the limit, as I'll have to guess which pieces need to be cut for those sections.

The sliver of tongue that Gron found fits perfectly into a section at chin level. Handling it again makes me squirm. All reddish-brown, and those tiny taste buds stippled on the surface. Just like the previous time, my mouth floods with saliva, and I swallow again and again. It leaves a salty tang behind—the taste of the sea.

I reach for my water bottle and rinse, but the taste refuses to budge. It leaves me feeling queasy, unnerved and afraid, and reminds me of the reverend's notes that spoke of the demon in the window stealing the power of speech from the couple who were about to be married.

For the time being I will leave the rest of the tongue. Not only will it be almost impossible to find the right colored glass among the boxes Hargreaves brought, but minute detail such as the taste buds will require hand-painting, and I can't bear the thought of tackling it yet. It's not that I don't enjoy adding those details; in fact, it's one of my favorite parts of the process, but... that tongue!

I finish the bottle of water and swallow two Aspirin in an attempt to alleviate the throbbing in my temples and the heat from the rash that has now spread to my neck and chest. If things don't improve soon, I'll have to make an appointment to see the G.P.

The boxes of glass remain closed beneath the arch of the window. The late afternoon sun weeps through the Perspex sheet Christian installed and casts a watery light on their lids. It's 16:20, according to the phone. Enough time to get a little more done before I finish for the day. I'm not paid an hourly rate, so it doesn't matter what time I work till, although I wouldn't want to drive the country lanes in the dark, not with them being so narrow. But nightfall is around ten o'clock at this time of year.

I take a craft knife and slit open the tape on the other two boxes, then remove the polystyrene packaging from all three. What lurks within is a jeweled feast. Now, where to begin?

The segments are all in good condition and have been thoroughly cleaned. No moss or dirt remains, not even a scrap of grout or old leading. This will save me some considerable time and make choosing the best glass for the remainder of the panel easier.

If I lay the contents of the boxes out tonight, in color-coded rows, I'll be able to start making the cuts tomorrow.

By the time I finish, the altar resembles the inside of a kaleidoscope, albeit a giant-sized one. I'm like a kid in a candy store, undecided which to choose and unsure whether making a decision will even be possible.

I turn back to the stencil, remove a segment from the deity's cloak, and hold it towards the light. Then I walk my fingers along the row of cobalt and bronze shades, selecting those I think will match. Decisions made, I take them outside, just to be certain. Daylight is best for comparing glass, and at this hour there's plenty left.

It's such a thrill to discover I've made the right choices. Both the original and the reclaimed pieces are a perfect match. Uncanny! How on earth did Hargreaves manage to acquire such identical pieces? Is there a chance he had harbored them all this time, or, as he suggested, did whoever created this window simply source the glass from the same glassblower? In the light of day, logic reins and persuades me the latter is more likely.

I annotate my choices with the number I coded for the deity's robe and return inside to start on a new section.

By seven-thirty, I've made matches for all the major elements of the design. From cloak to skin, bony growths to background. All that remains are the deity's facial features, including the tongue, and the minor figures.

As the evening chills and the sun dips on the horizon, I pack my bag and leave. I amble down the path, and a colony of pipistrelles swoop from the bell tower, darting across the lane and back again. Swift as lightning and with pinpoint accuracy, they dive within touching distance of me before whisking back to their roost, laden with moths and midges. As nocturnal creatures their day is just beginning, while mine should be drawing to an end. Except it isn't. Despite my aching head and burning skin I cannot rest, for the sketchbook and photographs await my scrutiny.

THIRTEEN

COPPERSGATE WOODS IS bathed in shadow as I climb the hill. A glance in the rearview mirror reminds me of the first time I spied it and the relief I had felt after assuming I was lost. So much has happened over the last few weeks that the memory of my first glimpse of the church seems like a lifetime ago. Another world.

Over dinner—a microwaved pasta bake—I sit with the sketchbook beside me and study the triple interlocked ovals on the front. It reminds me of the triquetra—the Celtic trinity knot. I turn the page, expecting to see another Celtic pattern. Instead, I see a sketch of an ear, malformed and twisted, as though someone has made it from clay only to pummel it with their fist. The charcoal medium against the pulpy paper gives it texture, a shadowed pinna, a swollen lobe.

So this is an artist's sketchbook then. But whose? I can't imagine Reverend James drawing such a thing, but perhaps he dabbled in illustration as well.

The next image is a hand, fingers splayed. Bony knuckles, riddled with arthritis. The third page depicts a section of chest, male I believe, since there's no sign of breast tissue. Flaccid pectorals, the skin wrinkled and sagging, but it's the nipple that makes me squirm in my seat. Areola shaped like an amoeba, the nipple itself distended and pocked with scabs. I put down my fork and push the plate away.

Page after page portrays a vile body part. A boxer's nose, flattened and pitted. A lipless gaping maw for a mouth. The more I see, the more I'm convinced that this is not the work of a church minister, especially not one as afraid of the demon as Reverend James. Unless this was his way of expressing his fear.

The final sketch is that of an eye socket, the brow bone furrowed and deep, the lid closed and the skin dewy, as though wet. I touch the paper, expecting it to be sticky.

I am disappointed, but not surprised, to find no name. I mean, who names their sketchbook? I would dearly love to know who it belongs to though.

The remainder of my dinner goes in the bin. I have lost my appetite for both the food and these sketches.

Instead, I pull up the photos I took of the crypt.

The first is of the etching—or the doppelganger, as Reverend James referred to it. The flash has served its purpose. Zoomed out, there is no doubt that this is a version of the rubbing I made of the leaded window. Some lines are faint, faded with time and disguised beneath mineral deposits, but I can make out the bony protrusions on the skull and shoulders, the short neck, and the hideously long tongue.

Why would someone repeat the design from the window on the crypt wall?

Head in hands as I lean over the image, I consider the conundrum. My assumption has been that the etching is a copy of the window, but what if the etching came first? Perhaps the wall served a purpose, a sketchbook being too small to work out the overall window. In that case, whoever designed the window might have used the crypt as their studio…

I shiver at the thought. Imagine spending that amount of time down there in the dark. I picture the space lit by candles, shadows dancing on the calcic walls. Atmospheric, no doubt, but a space I could never work in.

I close my eyes and try to remember the scale of the etching. It is difficult to judge, as the height of the crypt was far lower than that of the chancel. The window is seven feet tall, and the figure, or demon, a little shorter. The etching and the window are an approximate match, I think.

I zoom in, picking out specific parts. Here and there the surface is scored. The reverend's chisel perhaps? The features are best viewed from afar since the etching is somewhat crude and lacking in detail. My guess is that whoever created this did so to see what the overall effect might look like if it were made into a stained-glass window.

I switch to the photograph of the words on the entrance wall, words I now believe were written by Reverend James. They are faint but legible: *Beware of he who shines in the light, for he is the devil incarnate.* The poor man must have been driven to the brink of insanity by all that he witnessed.

The rest of the photos are of the wall with the scribbles. As far as I can tell, all of the words were written by the same hand: same cursive letters, same tool—a pencil I think, though the marks have faded with time. There are incriminatory words: *Persecutor! Spawn of the devil!* But pleading words, too, which make me pity his state of mind. *God, help me,* and, *Why am I forsaken?* among them.

There are also simple line drawings here and there: a crucifix, a bird, which I think is a dove, and an outline of the sun with an eye at its center, its pupil missing. This does not seem drawn by the hand of an artist, and certainly not the same hand that drew in the sketchbook.

I brew a pot of coffee, then curl up on the sofa with the parish register.

Baptisms and deaths. I read down the columns of names and dates, skimming over them and finding nothing of note, until an entry leaps out at me:

Name: Jonathan Hargreaves.

Birth: August 4th, 1812.

Baptism: August 26th, 1812.

Names of the Parents: Mother—Lydia Manning, Father—Unknown

Names are often passed down from generation to generation, and while the name Jonathan is common, the surname Hargreaves is less so. Illegitimate children were frowned upon back then, so I imagine it was tough for women such as Lydia.

Lydia Manning… The name rings a bell. *Lydia…Lydia.* Of course! The blind woman who knew that the carrot cake tasted just like my mother's. Do people in this town keep the names of their ancestors? And does this mean Lydia and Hargreaves are related?

If the father was unknown, why did the child not take his mother's surname? Is this yet another coincidence? If so, I have to admit, they seem to be stacking up.

The name Hargreaves sends me along another path to see if this name appears again, later on in the register, but despite a thorough search I am left disappointed. I cannot find anyone else named Jonathan Hargreaves in the register, neither in the baptisms nor deaths. In fact, the surname Hargreaves is not mentioned again.

The register goes as far as 1900, which would mean this child would have to have lived beyond the age of eighty-eight for his death not to be recorded. Unusual for someone to live to that age back then, but not impossible. Does this mean that he fathered no children either? There is also the possibility that he moved out of the district and had a family and was buried elsewhere.

For now, I must leave this puzzle and go to bed. I have a busy day ahead of me tomorrow.

FOURTEEN

THE NEXT MORNING when I arrive back at the church, Jess's van is already parked outside and I breathe a sigh of relief.

Jess, Luke, and Jordan lean against the wall, awaiting my arrival. "Hope I haven't kept you guys waiting?" I say. If I'd known they were coming I'd have got here earlier. I hurry up the path and unlock the door. "I guess you don't have a key."

"It's all right; we only just got here," Jess says, rubbing her eyes and yawning. "Should be finished by around lunchtime."

They jostle each other about, enjoying a bit of banter, before disappearing into the crypt, leaving me to continue where I left off last night. A hundred and seventy segments will need to be cut from the reclaimed glass, which will be quite a challenge.

By mid-morning, I've matched, annotated, and stenciled all the missing pieces to the best of my ability, aside from a specific few. The deity's facial features: its heavy brow, malformed ears, deep-socketed eyes, will need some consideration, so I work on the cloak and shoulders first. I also need to consider how the minor figures will look.

It's a shame the piece in the bottom right corner of the panel is missing, because that's where the original window designer would have inscribed his or her name. I could inscribe my own name, but signing it seems fraudulent. After all, I did not design the piece; I only restored it. *Tap, tap, tap.* The crow has returned and is intent on attacking the glass.

I hurry to the window. Black beady eyes stare in at me. It taps and taps with its equally black beak.

"Shoo! Go away!" I rap on the glass, and the bird takes flight, but not without issuing a loud *craa!*

Now that I can focus again, I can go back to work. I lay out the annotated card stencil pieces on the glass and stick them down. With my glass cutter and a jar of cutting oil at the ready, I make roads around each piece then break the glass, one edge at a time. Next, I run the wheel of the glass cutter along an edge and tap-cut until all the pieces are separated and sit on individual glass islands.

Since a curve is the hardest cut to make, I do those first, then work on the rest of the section. Pliers and nippers complete the cuts.

Now for the process I enjoy most: grinding. There's something therapeutic about running the glass along the grinding bit, and the perfectly smooth finish one gets from grinding is well worth the effort.

With my safety glasses on and hair wrapped in a shower cap, I set the grinder to face the window and begin. A ruckus behind me makes me turn around. Jess and the boys are gathered around the altar, staring at the half-complete panel.

I switch off the grinder and swipe my hands down the front of my apron to remove most of the water before joining them.

"What the actual fuck?" Jess says, mouth agape.

"I know, crazy isn't it?"

"Like…what's a thing like that doing in a church?" she says.

Luke sticks out his tongue and wiggles it close to her ear, making a slurping sound.

She flips him across the chest. "Fuck off, Luke. I'm not joking. Thing's hideous." She's grinning though. All three of them are.

"Reckon the real thing lives down in the crypt," Jordan says. "He's had his eye on us the whole time, I bet. He'll be reporting back to Hargreaves on whether we did a tidy job or not."

Jess leans over the panel to take a closer look. "Seriously though, whoever thought it was a good idea to design this for a church must have been off their rocker." She shudders. "Gives me the heebie-jeebies."

"Hey, Robin," Luke says, "why don't you give him a pair of purple glasses, for a laugh, like."

We roar with laughter.

Once we've calmed down, Jordan asks, "Christian seen it yet?"

I shake my head. "Nah, I haven't seen him since he helped me remove the window, but he'll be back next week to do some plaster-boarding—if the stuff ever gets delivered, that is. The window should be ready to install by then. I can't wait to see their faces."

"Aw, wish I could see his reaction when he does," Jordan says. "Reckon he'll freak."

It crosses my mind some of them might be local, and may even know something about the history of the church. "You guys live around here?"

"Only him," Jess says, pointing to Luke who is leaning over the panel, examining the face."

"Yeah," he says. "Just outside Bilbury. Brought up on a farm. You?"

I shake my head. "I'm not from around here. Do you know much about this church?"

He straightens, and folds his hands behind his neck, yawning. "Nah, not the churchy type myself, but my gran used to come here many years ago. She mentioned it the other day. Reckons the old vicar was a bit of a nutter." He sniffs.

"In what way?" Both Jess and Jordan have turned their attention back to the panel, but my interest is piqued.

"Dunno, really. She just said he started hearing voices and stuff. That's all I know." He shrugs.

"Did she say what happened to him? How did he die?"

He shrugs again. "I didn't ask."

I accept the fact that I'll glean no more information from him. Nevertheless, his words confirm what the reverend wrote in his notebook. Question is, was it really all in the reverend's mind, or did something more sinister happen?

Once the three of them have disappeared into the crypt, I get back to grinding the rest of the glass sections, hoping to position the majority of them before I leave work today. I really want the window ready to install when the boys arrive on Monday.

The more finished pieces I place within the design, the more alive the deity seems. It starts to trick my senses, encouraging me to imagine that the folds of its robe feel like silk rather than glass, and that the bony growths along its collarbone and shoulder hurt when I press them into position. I shake off the sensations. The reverend's writing has got to me, that's all, and I've allowed my imagination to take flight.

Beneath my feet, the others move about in the crypt. It's somewhat comforting knowing I'm not alone. The chancel is a mortuary, cold and clinical. The chemicals in the glue smell like formaldehyde, reminding me that what I am doing is preserving not only a work of art but an image of a deity—one that drove a man insane.

When a vehicle pulls up, I pause my work and face the door to the narthex, waiting to see who it is.

There is a flash of cream linen as Hargreaves passes it by without entering the nave. He must be here to see the builders, not me. I get back to work, assuming he'll pop in later to see how I'm getting on.

Raised voices from below make me pause again. I listen and wait. I'm unable to make out what's being said, but I sense tension seeping up through the floor.

Soon after, Hargreaves passes by again, this time on his way out. His movements are swift and give me the impression he is annoyed about something. I think of the loot I have stolen, picture the books on my kitchen table, and my face burns hot. Does he know they're missing? If he has accused my work colleagues of theft, I will have to come clean.

A minute or so later, Jess stomps down the aisle, her face like thunder.

I swallow hard, certain she is about to have a go at me, but instead she heads towards the sink and tosses her empty mug into the bowl. "Fucking nutter," she says, rinsing the mug and spraying water all over the draining board.

I'm almost afraid to ask. "What's up, Jess?"

She waves the dripping mug at me while wiping the other hand down the front of her overalls. "Had a go at me for breaking through that fucking wall. I told him it was ready to fall down of its own accord, but he wouldn't have it."

"Oh my God, really?" The relief is immense, but I try not to show it.

"We've damp-proofed the floor in the second chamber, and now the fucker's refusing to pay for the extra work. Says he wanted the wall left alone. I swear to god! There's no pleasing some people." She stands feet wide apart and arms folded. A formidable character when riled. "Anyway, we're off."

In the distance I hear the boys carrying tools out to the van, their voices subdued, like children who've been told off. She nods towards the panel that lies inert on the altar and pulls a face. "Best of luck with that ugly thing. It was nice knowing you."

Before I have chance to reply, she marches down the aisle with her nose in the air.

"Nice knowing you too, Jess." My voice is subdued. When she slams the door behind her, my energy drains.

I find it difficult to focus after seeing Jess so upset. I try not to blame myself, to accept that none of it was my fault, but when you've been brought up to believe everything that goes wrong is your fault, it's not easy to switch off. I sit on the altar steps and take a few deep breaths, wondering why Hargreaves would not have wanted the chamber opened up. Surely it's best that the whole floor is damp-proofed, not just part of it? Had he known there were secrets concealed behind that wall? He couldn't possibly know about them...unless he'd been in the chamber prior to it being bricked up.

What was it the reverend had written? *I believe in my heart he is in league with the demon in the window.*

He couldn't mean Hargreaves, could he?

I tell myself to stop being silly, that he's just a quirky old man, a man who has been polite and helpful in his dealings with me. And in any case, I'll be out of here in a few days' time. Gone for good.

Despite the pep talk, I find it hard to get back in the groove when I settle back down to work. The majority of the deity's tentacled tongue still needs attention, but I hesitate to work on this section, even though my nervousness makes me feel silly. Perhaps I should have got this part done while the others were here.

I force myself to begin, and soon immerse myself in the task, but the more pieces I place, the more real the tongue seems. Each sliver feels warm in my hand, more pliable than a shard of glass should be. I persuade myself that it's just my imagination, just the residual heat from the grinder. Yet…I sense the muscle beneath the surface, the connective tissue, engorged with blood. It makes me sick to the stomach. Saliva pumps to my mouth and I break out in a sweat. I'm not sure I can stand it any longer.

I'm grateful when, just after four o' clock, a delivery truck pulls up and draws me away from the work for a moment. I show them into the nave, sign the invoice, then drop Christian a text to say the supplies have arrived.

By five o'clock, I've finished cutting all the main pieces and positioned them. Now I can think about how the minor figures should look.

Before doing so, I take a well-earned break and sit outside, enjoying the late afternoon sun. Being among such peaceful surroundings helps to focus my mind. I sit on the wall, listening to the birds singing and leaves rustling, and soon I'm visualizing the characters that will complete the piece. I picture the scene…

Each profiled figure stands with their head tilted towards the deity, their hands folded as if in prayer. This I gleaned from the stencil. But something tells me the figures need to contrast with one another, as if the whole gamut of a population are in awe of the creature.

The stencil suggests three men and three women. Vague faces float in my vision. A gray-haired old lady, a redhead with an immaculate bob, and an elderly man wearing a tatty straw hat. There's something familiar about the three characters in my mind's eye, and yet I can't quite pin down their features. I won't need to worry too much, because all six stand side-on. The remaining three are less ready to reveal themselves, but I feel confident they will soon. At least now I have somewhere to start.

The old crow arrives with a great flurry of wings and perches itself high in the yew tree. *Craa*, it calls. *Craa, craa!* It reminds me to check on the glass it had pecked at earlier. I hope it hasn't scratched it. I wander across to the window. There, on the stone sill, something glistens—a sliver of mirror. Did the crow drop it, or has it left me a gift? I pick up the sliver, mindful of the sharp edges, and slip it into my pocket to dispose of safely, then head back inside to continue working.

For the old lady's hat and coat, I select black glass with a slight texture, like woolen fibers. I love using black glass here and there. It lends the design a touch of the medieval, and since there is hardly any black, I feel able to incorporate it without it being too dominant. Silver-gray to represent her hair. The gray glass has a lined texture, which, when painted with a few highlights and lowlights, should look like real hair. A ripple of joy surges through me. This haul of reclaimed glass is proving to be such a lucky find. Deciding on such elements are the most creative parts of the process and are what give me most pleasure.

For her skin, I select a pinkish opal shade, one with minute flecks of the palest brown. A perfect representation of age spots. A wrinkled eye and a hint of lip can be painted on later when I add the finishing touches.

A bright copper shade of glass for the red-headed woman's hair, and a creamy-white for her blouse. I want these figures to bring some life to the piece and stand out against the brown and yellow background. Although small in stature, I feel they are a key element of the overall design.

The straw-colored glass with a grainy texture will suit the old man's hat perfectly. For his skin, I choose the same shade as the old woman's, but his clothing must be less formal than that of the two women. I sense that the original artist depicted him as a man who had spent his life doing physical labor, in the fields, perhaps. I rummage among the slivers until I find an off-white shade – perfect for a peasant's shirt—and a tweedy shade of brown for his breeches. It's important to remember the style and fashion of the period in which the window was made and to forget about modern fashion.

My fingers walk the colored trail, considering what to choose for the final female. They stop at a buttercup shade, and I wince. With so much yellow in the background I wanted to steer clear of this color family, but the pull of the glass makes the decision for me. At least it's cheerful, I suppose; and the sun, when it hits, will look incredible through it. For her hair I choose deep mahogany, which will contrast well with the buttercup yellow. Some of the decisions I'm making seem intuitive rather than reasoned.

Two figures remain, but both feel problematic. My head suggests one thing; my gut another. In the end, I go with my gut and select the sombre vestments of a church minister for one figure, and a swirled gray glass for his hair. I feel uncomfortable with my decision. It does not seem fitting for a man of the cloth to stand in praise of such a deity. Still, I cut the pieces and lay them in place on the design to see how well they suit.

No, Robin, you've made the wrong decision.

I try to lift them out, but they refuse to move. My fingertips fumble and pluck at the edge of the glass, but the pieces will not relinquish their grip. Who is in charge here, me or the window?

I cannot even think about the final character right now. I need fresh air and a change of scenery.

When I step outside, I realize how late it is. The sky is bruised lavender. Here and there it blushes crimson. The air is thick and silent; even the birds are home to roost, all except for a little owl, who lets out a plaintive cry deep in the woods. I study the black silhouettes of the trees, their elongated shadows at ninety degrees on the ground.

Night will fall quickly; I need to get a move on if I want to be out of the narrow lanes before dark. I go back inside, switch off the lights in the church, and lock up.

As I navigate the winding roads, my thoughts return to the sixth and final figure. In my mind, I see a middle-aged man whose looks are nondescript—the kind of man who would blend in with the crowd—and yet the more I consider him, the more I sense a quality that's hidden from view.

I pull in at the petrol station to grab some milk and a few bars of chocolate. I'm in need of a carbohydrate-laden pick-me-up right now. Damn the guilt trip that is bound to follow.

Back home, I check my phone and find a text from Jules suggesting we meet for Sunday lunch. My heart sinks. I enjoyed the few hours we spent together the other week, but after working hard to complete the window, I had hoped to spend the weekend doing nothing other than relaxing. Besides, what will she make of my rash? She knows I've suffered from hives in the past, but I hate being seen in public when my skin looks like this.

Don't be such a bore, I tell myself. You're twenty-three years old, for Christ's sake! You should be out partying. And yet I can't help it. I'm exhausted. Both mentally and physically drained. The intensity of this project has sapped every ounce of strength.

I know that having cut myself off from my family means I need to protect what few friendships I have, and the more I say no to people the more likely they are to lose interest in remaining friends with me, but the simple truth is, I've never been a social butterfly. I enjoy my own company.

I put the kettle on before texting her back to suggest we meet the weekend after instead. I pretend I have to work on Saturday to get the window finished, which is not necessarily a lie, because at the rate I'm going I might well need to put in a few hours over the weekend.

When she agrees, the knot in my chest loosens a little. However, despite feeling exhausted, I find it impossible to relax. My head is full of angst. I respond to a few work-related emails and send quotes for two prospective jobs, but time and again, my mind returns to the stained-glass window.

Another microwaved meal will serve as supper. I don't even bother to transfer it to a dish.

I pick up Reverend James's notebook, again arrested by the line on the first page: *Something sinister stirs within these walls. Something ancient.*

It is true that both the reverend and I have experienced strange happenings at the church, but logic demands it is because of the setting. I mean, how much more atmospheric a place could you find than an ancient church in the middle of a wood?

That line though…

I realize now that I cannot destroy the deity, for it is not within my power. It has lived too long and grown too powerful. And those eyes! Blind, and yet all-seeing!

Every pore of my being empathizes with his sentiment. I read the sentence over again, the image of the deity sharp in my mind's eye. And in that moment, I see it…the glass for the deity's eyes must be white.

FIFTEEN

AFTER ANOTHER SLEEPLESS night, I park the van beneath the bough of the yew, which I swear has grown already since Gron cut it. I am anxious about what lies in wait inside the church. A branch of the yew snags my hair as I enter the gate, and I turn to see it has plucked out two or three blonde strands. It dangles them from its fingers like golden thread. A stolen gift. I could take it as an omen and leave right now, but that would be cowardly. Besides, the stone-hearted building wears an auspicious coat of sunshine this morning and once again lures me with the promise of treasure within.

Who you kidding, Robin? You could no more renege on this project than declare your family innocent.

The deity lies dormant on the altar, just as I left him last night. The morning sun showers him in glory, warming his fetid flesh with a pinkish hue and highlighting his cobalt cloak with flecks of electric blue. With a little galvanism, I swear the creature would spring to life, but without his terrible tongue, and with two holes where his eyes should be, he looks rather harmless. Like a lion that has lost its teeth.

I stand there for a minute or so, admiring the majesty of the panel, and all terror drains from my limbs. *It's just an image, Robin. A depiction in glass of mankind's fear of the punishment that might await him, should he sin.* Those would be my father's words, I know, and I hate myself for thinking in the same way he would. Can we ever escape the constraints of our upbringing? Or are we bound by them to some degree, no matter how hard we struggle to undo the rope's knots?

To distract myself, I turn my attention to choosing the slivers of glass for the sixth and final character within the scene. Determined to avoid all shades of brown, I walk my fingers along the rows of blue and gray, the maroon and then the green, but none feel right. The middle-aged man demands to be clothed in brown, and there is nothing I can do about it. Everything about him is brown, from his lightly tanned skin to his brogues, and within minutes my choices are made.

I make the cuts and finish assembling all six figures around the deity to check I'm happy with the overall effect. Now all I need do is add the suggestion of facial features and highlight parts of their clothing, and the figures will be complete. The painting will need to be carried out back at the studio, where I can access my lightbox and, more importantly, my kiln, so that the paint fuses to the glass and becomes permanent.

I sit on the altar step, contemplating what to do next. Tiredness has made me a little indecisive, which is not like me. I could try to wrap things up here by midday and spend the afternoon and evening back at the studio. That way every single piece would be ready to fit tomorrow, in time for me to start work on the leading and soldering.

I remember, then, how the slivers of glass I cut for the minister seemed unwilling to be removed from their position on the stencil. Ridiculous, I know, because they were merely placed there, not glued. I roll up my sleeve and flex my fingers, ready to do battle. But today the pieces issue no protest. I must have imagined it. One by one, I remove the pieces I chose for the six minor figures and annotate each by numbering and adding notes to a corresponding paper rubbing. Back at the studio, I'll be able to add detail to each piece with precision.

I'm about to repeat the process with the slivers of tongue when my phone beeps.

It's a text from Christian: *Hi Robin, thanks for letting me know the materials arrived. Looks like we'll be stuck on this job until next Wednesday at least, but I haven't forgotten the window. See you Monday at 8, unless you need more time.*

It's Thursday, so as long as everything goes to plan, the window should be ready by then. I have another job lined up for the middle of next week. Just the usual suburban front door, but when I make a promise, I like to keep it. I'll miss this place though. I'll miss it like hell.

I text back: *Great stuff! See you Monday!*

I turn my attention to the deity.

The only thing left to do is select the appropriate shade of white for its eyes and make a final decision regarding the corner section, where the artist's signature should go.

I pick up piece after piece of glass, holding each towards one of the diamond-leaded windows to see how it will look when natural light shines through. If the deity is blind, the pieces need to be semi-opaque. Yes, I can shade them back in the studio, but choosing the right type of glass to begin with is vital. I sift through piece after piece, but none are suitable. I am sorely disappointed. Until now, every piece has been a match made in heaven, but the glass for the deity's eyes eludes me. Such a vital part of the design too. Not one of the slivers offers the right opacity. The sky turns black. Great moody clouds have rolled in from nowhere. A minute ago, the sky had been clear, apart from the odd cloud dotted here and there.

The day has been warm and sultry, so I suppose a good old downpour is needed to clear the air.

A rumble of thunder, closer this time, almost above my head. I poke my nose outside. Electric air, pungent with ozone. It seems I am in Frankenstein's laboratory, and the lightning is waiting to reanimate the deity. Fat raindrops plop against my skin, and the sky is the color of murder. As I watch, a streak of lightning splits the sky in two, right above the yew tree.

Craa! The crow sits in the yew, shaking its head. Afraid of the storm, no doubt.

I'm about to close the door and head back inside when another lightning bolt strikes, illuminating the whole graveyard in silver. Something glints in the tree, at the edge of the crow's nest.

Craa! Craa, craa! The bird flaps its wings and hops about, spooked by the storm. Or is it?

Rain falls heavily now, and the parched grass sizzles as it quenches its thirst. *You must never stand under a tree during a lightning storm, Robin.* It's Pappi's voice I hear, the voice of reason, but it is drowned out by the storm. The storm that surges through me, stealing my sanity.

Because I know, without a shadow of doubt, what lies hidden within the old crow's nest. No heed for Pappi's words, I rush outside into the storm. Bullets of hail pelt my skin and my hair is soon sodden, but I hardly notice. I have one goal, and that is to persuade the crow to part with its treasure.

It eyes me from the nest, head tilted to one side. Each surge of wind ruffles its feathers; each flash of lightning flaunts its iridescence: indigo, lavender, copper and gold. I stand beneath the bough, hands folded in prayer and head raised. "Please, crow. I need what you have within your nest. I'll give you anything in exchange for it. Anything at all!"

It turns away, a snooty gesture. *Craa*, it says. *Craa, craa!* The thought of having to knock down its nest crosses my mind, but it's the last thing I want to do. I am certain now that the hair clip and the sliver of mirror were offered to me as gifts.

Another flash of lightning, another twinkle from the nest. The air is rife with ozone.

Rain soaks my face, mingling with my tears. I'm exhausted and desperate. I plead again, and the crow turns its head towards me, stretches its neck and shakes its tail. Then it picks up the sliver of glass and holds it in its beak for several seconds, as if considering, before dropping it at my feet.

My sobs turn to joy as I stoop to pick it up. "Thank you, crow. Thank you, thank you!"

Before I have time to examine it, the crow dips its head back into its nest, then leans out and drops another piece of scavenged treasure.

Craa, it says, lifting its head skyward. *Craa, craa!*

And just like that the storm abates, and in the palm of my hand lie two glass slivers, both white and perfectly opaque. A little dirty, but nonetheless perfect. My heart leaps with joy.

The sun peeps out from behind a dark cloud, and something twinkles on the ground. It looks like another sliver, partially buried and concealed within matted twigs and moss. I pocket the white segments and, with thumb and forefinger, tug at the hidden sliver until it breaks free of the earth.

The sliver is the color of caramelized toffee and engraved with a word, but it's too dirty to read.

I dash indoors, shivering and soaked to the skin, and hurry to the sink.

A squirt of detergent, warm water, and a soft cloth, and the signature reveals itself. One word: *Nyarlathotep.*

The name is vaguely familiar, though I haven't a clue why. My heart races and my palms are slick with sweat. I haven't felt this excited in a long time.

I take the three slivers over to the stencil to check they fit, though I don't doubt it for one moment. Perfect!

Drunk on adrenalin, I strip off my overalls and put the kettle on to make a tea.

While it's boiling, I pull up the online search on my phone and type in the name.

How can this be? According to Google, Nyarlathotep is a fictional character created by horror writer H.P. Lovecraft in 1920.

Nyarlathotep, the many-faced god, an agent of chaos, one who wanders the earth in search of followers.

Someone must have stolen a fictional character's name to hide their true identity.

I am sure the window was designed between 1880 and 1910, but if the poem titled "Nyarlathotep" wasn't written until 1920, as my search suggests, then the timing doesn't add up. Unless Lovecraft took the name from somewhere.

I search for prior uses of the name before his time, but everything points to him as the originator. The thrill of finding the missing pieces has turned into utter confusion.

The reverend's words come back to haunt me yet again: *Something sinister stirs within these walls. Something ancient.*

The kettle bubbles and steams, matching the energy in my brain. *Holy shit, what the hell have I got myself into?*

SIXTEEN

THE AFTERNOON IS spent in the studio, painting detail on the minor figures' features, stippling taste buds onto the tongue, and adding a few highlights here and there by foiling.

Hours later, with the shards put safely to bed in the kiln, I turn my attention to researching the artist's name. Instead of alleviating the surreal nature of it all, my searching draws me further and further into the realms of fantasy. I read "The Haunter of the Dark" and discover it features a three-lobed eye. My thoughts turn to the symbols on the gravestones and the drawing on the cover of the sketchbook. Could they represent a three-lobed eye? Regardless, no such symbol appears on the window itself. I should know. I've spent enough time piecing it back together.

Besides, the story wasn't written until 1935, so it couldn't be connected to the window.

Nevertheless, I research it a little further and discover the three-lobed eye may signify something that perceives things beyond our known senses, beyond the realm of our universe. I also see it referred to as *the eye of chaos*, appearing as a hieroglyph in Egyptian, Indian and Incan cultures.

A hieroglyph…What if the connection between the window and the artist's reference to Lovecraft lies in the deity's sense of perception? His ability to see beyond what is there. His ability to see inside us, just like Lydia.

The more I read, the more certain I am that there is a connection between the artist who designed the stained-glass window and the mystery surrounding the place. Nyarlathotep is said to not only appear in a thousand guises but also to strip a person of their sanity, reminding me of the poor Reverend James and the way in which he was driven insane.

Could Lovecraft have learned about the reverend and the mystery surrounding the church, through a friend's correspondence perhaps, and incorporated elements into his own writing? After all, isn't that what writers do? Take bits and pieces from here and there and make it their own?

The "The Haunter of the Dark" story had also featured a sinister cult called the Church of Starry Wisdom founded by a character named Professor Enoch Bowen. Perhaps Lovecraft used a real-life cult, and all its secrets, as the basis for his short story. But what was the tie to the window, if any?

By the time the clock approaches midnight, I am no longer capable of separating reality from fantasy or fact from illusion, and I've managed to convince myself that the reason the church's name was stripped from the building, as well as all record books, is because it too was named the Church of Starry Wisdom. How apt a name for a building set within such magnificent surroundings, one devoid of light pollution, where an astronomer might study the stars to their heart's content. However, it was not the stars that these cultists worshiped, but the Haunter of the Dark himself.

THE FOLLOWING MORNING, when I unload the kiln and see the fired shards of glass, an element of actuality re-emerges. They are shards of glass and nothing more. Inorganic solid matter that, regardless of how they are assembled, cannot breathe life into an image. I gather the pieces and pack them carefully before setting off for the church.

A busy day lies ahead. The last working day of the week before the boys are due to arrive and help me reinstall the panel. I need to stay sane and calm, or I could blow this project out of the water.

Yesterday's turbulent weather has calmed, and the church and its surroundings appear as innocuous as a wasp without a stinger. Even the old crow seems in a good mood. It sits on a high branch and sings a cooing song of welcome as I enter the gate.

I set to work, placing the last slivers of glass in the design. They fit like a glove, and I cannot wait to see how the window looks once it's leaded.

Just before ten-thirty, I hear Hargreaves' car pull up. I stop work and wait for him to enter, though I dread seeing him after all I've discovered. As much as I want to see the window finished, I cannot wait for it to be over so that I can move on.

He strides down the aisle, then stands in front of the altar. "Magnificent," he says, rubbing his hands in glee. "The eye pieces…, did you find them or cut them from the glass I brought?"

I shake my head. "You wouldn't believe me if I told you."

He frowns.

"Let's just say a friend of mine gave me a gift."

"I hope they're authentic."

"Yes, of course…I was wondering, what do you make of this?" I run my finger along the signature in the corner, watching him closely for any sign of duplicity.

He tries to read it aloud but has trouble pronouncing the name. He breaks it into syllables but places the emphasis on the first syllable instead of the second. "Nyarla...?"

"Nyarlathotep."

His face is blank, and he scratches his head. "Never heard of him. Is it foreign?" No change in pitch or expression, though I can't tell what's behind the glasses.

"You might say that. Actually, it's a fictional character from an H.P. Lovecraft story."

His forehead wrinkles. "How strange." He seems less interested in the signature than in the deity's eyes. His finger hovers over them again, forming a wavy line as it flows from one to the other, hypnotic, then he takes an audible breath and changes the subject.

"Anyway," he says, breaking into a smile. "I'm here to invite you to a little get-together. If you'll oblige, that is."

"A get-together?" I'm taken aback. I don't relish the thought of spending social time in his company.

"Yes. Tuesday morning, once the panel is back in its place. How would you feel about meeting a few members of the parish council here for an unveiling?"

He sees me hesitate.

"It'll be weeks before the builders finish." He sweeps a hand around the nave. "And I have to admit, I can't wait to see the expressions on the committee members' faces when they see what you've achieved." He gestures at the panel and grins, and a whiff of stale breath wafts in my direction, making me want to gag. Coffee and cigarettes. I hadn't imagined him to be a smoker.

Put on the spot, I can think of no excuse other than to say I have another job to attend, but that would only mean delaying the inevitable. Perhaps I should agree and get this whole thing behind me. I know how I am; it'll weigh heavy on my mind if I have to return weeks or even months in the future.

"All right. What time were you thinking?"

He hesitates and shuffles his feet. "Well," he says, "would you be willing to get here for sunrise? As the window faces directly east, I can only imagine how magnificent it will look when the morning light hits."

I rub the back of my neck. After all the stress of the last few weeks, I'd been hoping to have a lie-in on Tuesday before starting the new job the following day.

"Please," he says, his hands folded in front of him. "I'll pay you for the extra day. I just want the committee to appreciate the window at its finest, that's all."

How can I refuse? He seems rather desperate. "Okay. Tuesday it is.

He breathes a sigh of relief. "Thank you, thank you. Shall we say six o'clock? Oh, and do send me the invoice as soon as you're ready. I'm delighted with your work. Truly delighted."

It's not complete yet, and I'm surprised by how emphatic he is. Though of course I'm pleased. "Wait till you see it leaded. That's when it all comes together."

THE REST OF the day is spent leading and soldering, and by six o'clock my face burns red and my skin is parched. My fingers are sore and scorched here and there from the soldering iron, but the finished result is incredible, even if I say so myself. I wish I had the strength to lift the panel off the altar and prop it against the window opening, but it would probably break if I tried to lift it on my own. I will have to be patient and wait until Monday.

Hungry and exhausted, I cast my gaze around the room, taking in all my tools and equipment. I'll pop round tomorrow morning to pack my things and clean the place in readiness for Tuesday's unveiling. I don't want the committee to think me slovenly, the term my father often labeled me.

There is one thing I'm still unsure of, and that is what to do about the books. Do I hand them over and admit I've read them? It's the honest thing to do, but I don't think I have the courage. Should I keep them? But that would be stealing. The only other alternative is to bring them with me in the morning and secret them back into the crypt.

SEVENTEEN

CHRISTIAN AND THE boys breeze in like a breath of fresh air on Monday morning, but when they see the renovated panel their mouths fall open. Matt's words are identical to Jess's. "What the actual fuck?"

My mouth twitches. "So, what d'you think?"

All three stand around the altar, captivated by the image. Arnie scratches the bristles on his chin, while Christian runs a hand through his hair. None of them are able to steal their eyes away.

"I mean, it's amazing, and you've done an incredible job, but…" Christian says. "Fucking scary, man! Imagine looking at that thing while you take your vows."

His words break the ice and make us laugh. I'm close to snapping point today, what with the window being reinstalled and thinking about the books, so it's good to have some light relief.

"Right then," he says, "let's get to it. Don't drop this, boys, for Christ's sake."

Before they approach the panel, I stop them. "Do you mind wearing gloves? It's just I don't want fingerprints on the glass." I wiggle my fingers to show I'm already wearing mine. "Once the window's in, it'll be too high to clean without a ladder." I had prepared for this morning; I grab three pairs of gloves and pass them around. Not only will they help to keep the glass clean, but the rubber is textured and will help with grip.

My heart is in my mouth as we lift the panel, two of us on each side. The boys are anxious. I can tell by the way they fall silent. I've had a few tricky installations in the past, but none as delicate as this. This window has been a labor of love and has demanded more of me than any job I've ever done. Despite all the stress, the hives, and the headaches, I wouldn't have missed it for the world.

In less than an hour, and without a hitch, the window is safely installed in its frame. All four of us stand back to admire it. A lump sticks in my throat, and for an awful minute I think I might cry.

Christian puts a friendly arm around my shoulders and pulls me close, but I shrink back, embarrassed by the physical contact.

"Thank you, guys. I appreciate your help. I'll have to come back one day, once you've finished the interior work, and see how the place looks. I'm sure you'll do a grand job."

"Course we will," Christian says, winking at me. "Rightio, we'd better get going. See you again then, Robin."

Once they leave, I spend an hour or so alone with the window, switching various lights on and off and checking to see how it looks from outside as well as inside. The lancet windows on either side project elongated spotlights across the floor on either side of the deity, but it is the window's own reflection that fascinates me most. Almost twice the size of the real thing, and a perfect replica of the image, the reflection snakes its long tongue across the flagstones. The tongue is engorged with blood and speckled with tiny taste buds. I imagine it licking at the minister's heels, saliva wet and sticky. No wonder the image gave Reverend James nightmares.

The most mesmerizing aspect of the reflection is the deity's eyes. Milky-white and raised towards the stars, he is blind, yet all-seeing. A contradiction, and yet I know it's the truth. He sees me now, I'm certain. Reads my every thought.

I shudder, and the hairs on my arms stand proud.

Just one more task to complete before I head home: I must return the books to the crypt, and hope that the etching on the wall won't speak of my deception when it next sees Hargreaves.

WHEN I AGREED to meet at sunrise, I hadn't considered the narrow lanes. Twilight reigns as I drive through Bilbury, and only a few cars are already on the road. I wonder if the occupants might be members of the committee.

Snip 'n Tucker is in darkness. It seems a lifetime ago that I sat in the cafe, eating an exact replica of my mother's carrot cake. My throat constricts. I still haven't come to terms with the reality of not seeing any of my family again…not really. I make a left at the crossroads, then left again onto the unclassified road that eventually leads to Coppersgate Woods. The journey feels far less threatening now than it did a few weeks back; in fact, it feels familiar. If I had to, I think I could drive it blindfolded.

With cloudless skies overnight, the dawn is cool. It breathes its mist over the fields which settles just above the grass, making it disappear from sight. Dry-stone walls and boundary hedgerows seem to float a foot above ground.

The closer to the church I get, the more flustered I feel. I'm not good with strangers, and hate being the center of attention. I lower the car window to cool my face. Today, the hives are prominent. Despite doing all I can to camouflage them, they have gained the upper hand. Even the skin around my eyes and nose is raised.

The clock on the dashboard reads 05:50, which means I'm ten minutes early. My father would approve.

Two cars are already parked outside the church: Hargreaves' and another I don't recognize. I squeeze the van in beside the two cars and take a deep breath.

All the lights are on inside, though the windows are too high to spot anyone. The darkness of the woods jostles the sun for position, ensuring dawn will not arrive until the trees give it permission to do so. A lavender sky turns teal as I walk along the path, but the sun sits below the horizon.

The front door issues a deep moan as I enter, announcing my arrival. I wipe my sweaty palms on my jeans and walk through the narthex and into the nave.

In front of the altar stands Jonathan Hargreaves, a red-headed woman beside him. He waves when he sees me.

"Ah, Robin. Good to see you."

As I walk down the aisle, the redhead turns to face me, and I recognize her in an instant. The woman from the library—the rude one who refused to help me search for information about the church. My heart sinks.

"I was just telling Moira about my lucky find," Hargreaves says. "Would have cost us a lot more if we'd had to buy new glass."

Moira. The name tastes like cheap red wine on my tongue—bitter, with a hint of aniseed. Her white blouse is crisply ironed, just like her manner.

"You've done a marvelous job here," she says, handing me a glass of orange juice from a tarnished silver tray which rests on a side table. She does not seem to recognize me, or if she does, she hides it well.

"Thank you." I take a sip and swallow, grateful for the distraction.

"I must admit, when Jonathan said he'd employed a woman to do the job I had my doubts." Her smile reveals lipstick-stained teeth, and her ignorant comment frees my tongue.

"And why might that be?" There's a tremor to my voice, and my eyes are narrowed.

Her jaw is clenched. "Well, you know…the physical labor involved. I wasn't sure a woman could handle it." She pokes out her tongue and pretends to pick at something that has stuck to it, a hair perhaps.

I'm about to reply when the door creaks open and in walks Gron. I hadn't heard his van pull up, but I should have realized he'd be here, since he's on the committee. He wears the same old straw hat, and, in contrast to the librarian's, his shirt looks as if it has never been ironed.

Gron limps down the aisle, then stands hands on hips, gazing up at the window. I hold my breath and scan his face, keen to see his reaction. He reminds me so much of Pappi again—same limp, same demeanor. His eyes are rheumy, and I wonder if it's because he feels teary or if it's because of the cataracts. But why had I imagined him as lustful? My skin crawls at the memory, and I recall the words written by Reverend James: *It takes possession of our senses, causing us to hear what it wants us to hear, feel what it wants us to feel, smell what it wants us to smell.*

Before I have chance to assimilate their meaning, Gron speaks.

"Magnificent," he says, his voice breaking. "Truly magnificent." He seems unable to steal his gaze away from the window, which makes me all the more eager for sunrise.

The door opens again, and two women enter—one elderly, the other the right side of middle-age. The younger leads the older woman by the elbow. And then I see it: a white stick. Lydia! I wouldn't have guessed she'd be on the committee. Not at her age.

The closer they get, the more certain I am that I've met the younger woman too. Her hair is a bottle shade of mahogany, her gray roots beginning to show, but her pale-yellow blouse makes up for it.

"Ah," Hargreaves says, rushing to her side and taking Lydia's elbow. "So glad you could make it. Robin, meet Ava and my mother, Lydia." His mother? Dumbstruck, I fail to offer a greeting.

"I remember you," Lydia says. "The girl with the carrot cake." She chuckles, and a froth of spittle forms at the corner of her mouth.

Something feels off here. My sixth sense springs into action. I glance at the others. The librarian is bent over a plate of petite fours. Gron's gaze is still fixed on the window, as if it hypnotizes him. Ava fusses over settling Lydia on a chair.

I follow Gron's gaze. The dawn light creeps up the bottom half of the mosaic window, highlighting the deity's cloak, but it has not yet reached as far as the minor figures, his flock.

Hargreaves glances from window to wristwatch, clearly agitated.

His brow is furrowed, his upper lip beaded with sweat. He gathers himself and flashes a toothy smile. "Not long now. Just waiting for two more."

I gulp the rest of the juice. It curdles in my stomach. Never before have I felt this anxious, not even when I told my mother I never wanted to see her again. This is different. Surreal almost. At any moment, I expect to be whisked off my feet and tossed into the air. My head swims, and I feel as though I'm about to faint.

The door bursts open to reveal an old man, dressed head-to-toe in vestments. The hem of his black cloak sweeps the floor as he ambles down the aisle.

"Sorry I'm late," he says, dabbing at his brow with a white handkerchief. His breathing is erratic, as if he has been exercising, but his pallor is the color of maggots. "I couldn't park." He points back towards the door. "Had to park further down the lane and walk." His face relaxes a little when he sees the window.

"Welcome, welcome," Hargreaves says, beckoning him closer. "There's plenty of time, so don't worry."

Now that the minister is here, Hargreaves seems more at ease. I suppose this was the guest he most wanted to see, what with it being a church. Perhaps he has come to bless the window.

"Robin," says Hargreaves, "meet Reverend Peter James."

Impossible! Reverend Peter James died in 1995. A low murmur threatens to escape my lips, but I manage to stifle it. Instinct tells me to flee, but my conventional upbringing implores me to stay. *Manners, Robin,* my father whispers in my ear. My thoughts are incoherent, hissing like snakes.

A hush has fallen on the place. I glance around to find all eyes on me. No one smiles. Before I can decide what to do, the door creaks open.

"No." The single syllable slips from my lips, barely audible, and my knees buckle.

Surely my eyes deceive me.

He strides down the aisle, a strut, confident to the point of arrogance.

My father!

He frowns and wags his finger at me, but when he turns to address the others, he is all smiles. "I see you've met my daughter, Robin," he says. His face is tanned, swarthy, as if he has just stepped off a plane. It shows off his white teeth, which he paid through the nose to maintain. My vain, wolfish father. His grin reeks of insincerity. "But don't be fooled," he continues. "Despite her innocent appearance, she can be quite aggressive, just like the bird she's named after."

He has reached the foot of the chancel, close enough that, should I wish, I could reach out a hand and touch him.

I am a ventriloquist's dummy, unable to speak for myself. My whole life he has had this effect on me. What on earth is he doing here?

Only then do I notice what he is wearing. Brown brogues, a brown sweater, beneath which peeks a ridiculously wide tie.

Hargreaves steps towards him and places a hand on his shoulder, like an old friend. "I knew you'd come," he says.

This situation is absurd. A nightmare I am incapable of waking from. How can my father be here? My parents don't even have my address, never mind the address of this place.

I glance from one to the other, desperate for someone to come to my aid. I expect at any moment to wake up. Either that, or for someone to shout "surprise!" and declare the whole thing a joke.

"Tell me," Hargreaves says to my father, "are you proud of your daughter's work?" He gestures towards the window, just as the morning sun blesses the deity's torso with her finest rays.

My father opens his mouth but fails to reply.

The deity's reflection crawls along the stone floor towards Hargreaves, a doppelganger twice the size of the glass version and muted around the edges, as if bleeding into the stone.

My father's lips have turned blue, and his body stiffens. I watch in horror as the man who has thrived on control his whole life loses his dominion. A patch of urine spreads across his pants, pooling at his feet. He stares at Hargreaves, his mouth hanging open, and for a moment I think he is suffering a stroke. Pitiful, yes, but in truth I feel nothing but shock.

"Well?" Hargreaves says, "Aren't you going to answer?" The deity's reflection licks at Hargreaves' heels, while Hargreaves stammers in a mocking gesture at my father's dumb floundering. "Hmm," Hargreaves says. "It seems that for once you have nothing to say."

My father clutches his throat, then falls to his knees at his master's feet. Why summon him here though, if only to humiliate him?

One line dominates my thoughts, a line from the Bible: Oh, how the mighty have fallen.

Lydia rises from her chair without so much as a groan, and, one by one, all five guests congregate around Hargreaves. On his left stands the librarian, Gron, and the reverend; on his right, Ava, Lydia…and my father, who kneels.

"Stand!" Hargreaves demands.

And, though in agony, my father does as he is bidden. And now I see it.

The six figures stand in praise of the deity. Every item of clothing and even the color of their hair matches the glass I chose. How is this possible? The tableau before me is arranged exactly like the window, except instead of the beast, there stands Hargreaves.

I hear a pathetic moan. It takes a few seconds before I realize it's coming from me.

EIGHTEEN

A SWITCH FLICKS to green inside my head—a physical jolt of electricity as my body comes back to life. *Run, Robin...Run!*

I gasp a breath and turn towards the aisle, but at that moment the sun strikes the face of the beast in the stained-glass window, lighting the milky orbs of its eyes. They roam inside bone-white sockets, desperate to focus. His wandering eyes settle, and he sees me. His thoughts project across the altar straight into my brain. I clamp my hands over my ears, screw up my eyes so I don't have to witness it. The pain in my head is Thor's hammer; my hives a dragon's flame.

Open your eyes, he says, his words stern, and yet somehow...encouraging. *You have brought me back to life, and you must witness the fruits of your labor.*

Enraptured by the sound of his voice, I do as he says.

Hargreaves steps close to my father, and I blink as my father's form dissipates before me, blending into Hargreaves and ceasing to exist in his own right. At the last second, before he vanishes completely, he looks at me with disdain in his eyes, and I return the look with one of regret. Then the man who would be king becomes one with his master.

But this is no longer the Hargreaves I know. The deity's reflection creeps up Hargreaves' torso, turning his crumpled linen jacket into a kaleidoscopic cloak. Tumors protrude above his collarbone and his skull, and for a moment I think he's suffering from some disease. Then I realize the protrusions are the bony growths of the deity.

He issues a long moan, and his skin mottles. His eyes, no longer hidden behind mirrored glasses, roll back in his head, ghostly white.

The others move closer to him, drawn like moths to a flame, and slowly meld into his robes. There are no struggles, no anguished cries. I think of the writing on the tapestry at the cafe: *The worker bees protect the hive.* Subservient to the last.

Soon, Lydia, Ava, Gron, Reverend James, and the librarian, are all swallowed by the thing that is neither a man nor a god.

Were they ever really there?

It is the last logical thought I have before Hargreaves and the thing in the window become one.

The scent of the sea and the thrum of his heartbeat. The click of a jaw, his mouth opens, and the chancel fills with the stink of his breath. His tongue quivers, tasting the air—a serpent in a monster's maw. Beneath his robes, something squirms, sending subtle ripples along the cobalt cloth. The veins beneath his skin throb with life, and the growths on his chest and shoulders glisten silver with sweat.

He whispers his name: "*Nyarlathotep*," the word breathy and perfectly emphasized.

And my fear dissipates into thin air, taking the pain and discomfort that has plagued me these past weeks with it. I gaze towards the rafters and watch it float away like ice crystals on the wind. I look into his eyes and know what it is he wants.

Behind him, the window blazes, blinding me with its rays so that no image is visible. I turn my back to the altar so that I can see his face. His breath is a tempest, his engorged tongue a whip, and I am to be its willing victim.

"Be still, my love," I whisper. "Cease your thrashing, and I shall be yours."

My lips are receptive and my throat relaxed, though I am unprepared for the length of his tongue. My esophagus recoils instinctively, and I gag. His kiss is frenzied, probing and forceful; his heart beats rapidly against my breast.

But soon it is done. He is spent.

I WAKE TO a starlit sky. The Church of Starry Wisdom is flooded with candlelight, the stained-glass window lit from behind by the cool blue of the moon. His face is placid, peaceful. His tongue hangs limp. Clouds scud across the sky, animating his features with their shadows. No fervor in those bone-white orbs now, the fire is extinguished.

I kneel before him and bow my head in praise, my hands circling my warm belly, which is already beginning to swell.

Soon, the man with a thousand faces will have another. Perhaps I shall name him Niall, meaning *champion*. No one will be any the wiser.

From this day onward I shall do his bidding and gather his flock to this place, in readiness for his rebirth. After all, his old face was becoming a little ragged, a little worn around the edges. A little stuck in the past.

I walk down the aisle with the grace of a dancer, and as I cross the threshold, the old crow calls to me. *Craa!* it says. *Craa, craa!* It sounds as though it's apologizing for something, as if in relinquishing the glass, it bears some burden of guilt.

"Don't fret, crow," I whisper, palm pressed to abdomen, feeling the kick that is already strong. "Your gift has helped vanquish my solitude."

The moon shines bright on the headstones, picking out the three-eyed symbol on each of their faces. The final resting places of his old worshipers. I bid them farewell and step through the gate.

In the rearview mirror of the van, I study my reflection: calm, collected. My irises are stripped of color. They sparkle white as opals, but the gift of sight is still mine.

Believe me. I see everything.

ACKNOWLEDGMENTS

AS WRITERS WE spend the majority of our time alone, furiously bashing away at the keys until something acceptable takes shape before our eyes. The journey can seem a lonely one, and yet there are many who help us along the way.

First of all I would like to thank my husband, Tony. Without your encouragement and wisdom, this book would not exist. You are my first reader, my harshest critic, my best friend, and my life.

Immense thanks and appreciation to my publishers, Rob Carroll and Sadie Hartmann, for believing in this story. Your professionalism, hard work, and friendship along the way have meant so much.

To my editor, Marissa van Uden, for casting an incredible eye over the manuscript and helping me make it what it is today. I swear, in another life, you were an eagle!

A huge shout-out to my fellow writer and comrade, Tim McGregor, for your oh-so-supportive beta read of this novella and your continued support for my work. I truly cannot thank you enough.

To the horror community at large, of whom there are far too many to mention. You are all incredible and inspire me every day!

Last, but not least, to each and every reader, without whom our work would have no purpose. Sincere appreciation, always.

—Catherine McCarthy

ABOUT THE AUTHOR

CATHERINE MCCARTHY IS a spinner of silky stories with macabre melodies. When she is not writing, she may be found hiking the Welsh coast path or huddled among ancient gravestones reading Machen or Poe. Follow her on Twitter @serialsemantic.

Also Available or Coming Soon from Dark Matter INK

Human Monsters: A Horror Anthology
Edited by Sadie Hartmann & Ashley Saywers
ISBN 978-1-958598-00-9

Zero Dark Thirty: The 30 Darkest Stories from Dark Matter Magazine, 2021–'22
Edited by Rob Carroll
ISBN 978-1-958598-16-0

Linghun by Ai Jiang
ISBN 978-1-958598-02-3

Monstrous Futures: A Sci-Fi Horror Anthology
Edited by Alex Woodroe
ISBN 978-1-958598-07-8

Our Love Will Devour Us by R. L. Meza
ISBN 978-1-958598-17-7

Haunted Reels: Stories from the Minds of Professional Filmmakers curated by David Lawson
ISBN 978-1-958598-13-9

The Vein by Stephanie Nelson
ISBN 978-1-958598-15-3

Other Minds by Eliane Boey
ISBN 978-1-958598-19-1

Frost Bite by Angela Sylvaine
ISBN 978-1-958598-03-0

Monster Lairs: A Dark Fantasy Horror Anthology
Edited by Anna Madden
ISBN 978-1-958598-08-5

Chopping Spree by Angela Sylvaine
ISBN 978-1-958598-31-3

The Bleed by Stephen S. Schreffler
ISBN 978-1-958598-11-5

Free Burn by Drew Huff
ISBN 978-1-958598-26-9

The House at the End of Lacelean Street
by Catherine McCarthy
ISBN 978-1-958598-23-8

The Off-Season: An Anthology of Coastal New Weird
Edited by Marissa van Uden
ISBN 978-1-958598-24-5

The Dead Spot: Stories of Lost Girls
by Angela Sylvaine
ISBN 978-1-958598-27-6

When the Gods Are Away by Robert E. Harpold
ISBN 978-1-958598-47-4

Grim Root by Bonnie Jo Stufflebeam
ISBN 978-1-958598-36-8

Voracious by Belicia Rhea
ISBN 978-1-958598-25-2

Abducted by Patrick Barb
ISBN 978-1-958598-37-5

Darkly Through the Glass Place by Kirk Bueckert
ISBN 978-1-958598-48-1

The Threshing Floor by Steph Nelson
ISBN 978-1-958598-49-8

Other Books in The Dark Hart Collection

Rootwork by Tracy Cross
ISBN 978-1-958598-01-6

Apparitions by Adam Pottle
ISBN 978-1-958598-18-4

I Can See Your Lies by Izzy Lee
ISBN 978-1-958598-28-3

A Gathering of Weapons by Tracy Cross
ISBN 978-1-958598-38-2

Milton Keynes UK
Ingram Content Group UK Ltd.
UKHW010630140823
426838UK00004B/333